A CLASH OF KINGS

THE GRAPHIC NOVEL

VOLUME 1

GEORGE R. R. MARTIN

A CLASH OF KINGS

THE GRAPHIC NOVEL

VOLUME 1

ADAPTED BY LANDRY Q. WALKER

ART BY MEL RUBI

COLORS BY IVAN NUNES

LETTERING BY SIMON BOWLAND

ORIGINAL SERIES COVER ART

BY MIKE S. MILLER AND

COLORS BY NANJAN JAMBERI

BANTAM BOOKS · NEW YORK

Copyright © 2018 by George R. R. Martin

All rights reserved.

Published in the United States by Bantam Books, an imprint of Random House, a division of Penguin Random House LLC, a Penguin Random House Company, New York.

Bantam Books and the House colophon are registered trademarks of Penguin Random House LLC.

All characters featured in this book, and the distinctive names and likenesses thereof, and all related indicia are trademarks of George R. R. Martin.

ISBN 978-0-440-42324-9
Ebook ISBN 978-1-9848-1746-4

Printed in China on acid-free paper by RR Donnelley Asia Printing Solutions

randomhousebooks.com

9 8 7 6 5 4 3 2 1

Graphic novel interior design by Foltz Design.

Visit us online at www.DYNAMITE.com
Follow us on Twitter @dynamitecomics
Like us on Facebook /Dynamitecomics
Watch us on YouTube /Dynamitecomics
Instagram /Dynamitecomics
On Tumblr dynamitecomics.tumblr.com

Nick Barrucci, CEO / Publisher
Juan Collado, President / COO

Rich Young, Director of Business Development
Alan Payne, V.P. of Sales and Marketing

Joseph Rybandt, Executive Editor
Matt Idelson, Senior Editor
Anthony Marques, Associate Editor
Kevin Ketner, Assistant Editor

Jason Ullmeyer, Art Director
Geoff Harkins, Senior Graphic Designer

Cathleen Heard, Graphic Designer
Alexis Persson, Graphic Designer
Chris Caniano, Digital Associate
Rachel Kilbury, Digital Multimedia Associate

CONTENTS

A CLASH OF KINGS

THE GRAPHIC NOVEL

VOLUME 1

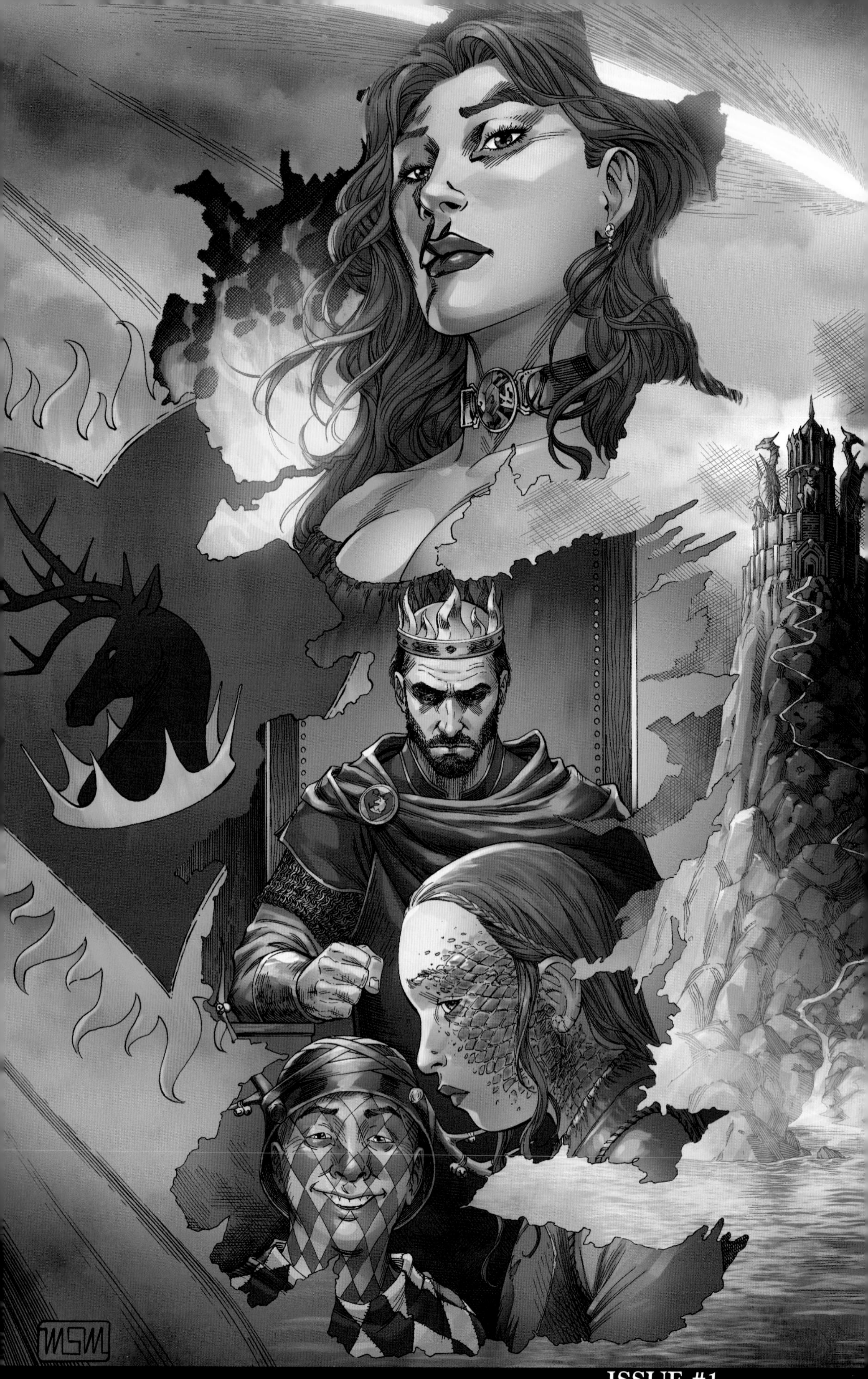

ISSUE #1

PROLOGUE

THE COMET'S TAIL SPREAD ABOVE THE CRAGS OF DRAGONSTONE LIKE A WOUND IN THE SKY.

THE COMET BURNED EVEN BY DAY NOW, WHILE PALE GREY STEAM ROSE FROM THE HOT VENTS OF DRAGONMONT BEHIND THE CASTLE.

AND YESTERMORN, A WHITE RAVEN HAD ARRIVED FROM THE CITADEL.

MAESTER CRESSEN...

...WE HAVE VISITORS.

HELP ME TO MY CHAIR...

WHAT DID IT ALL MEAN?

AH! WHO COMES TO SEE US SO EARLY, PYLOS?

CLANG-A-LANG CLONG

IT'S ME AND PATCHES, MAESTER.

PYLOS SAID WE MIGHT SEE THE WHITE RAVEN.

INDEED YOU MAY.

MAESTER PYLOS, DO ME A KINDNESS AND BRING THE BIRD DOWN FROM THE ROOKERY FOR THE LADY SHIREEN.

IT WOULD BE MY PLEASURE.

BONG-DONG CLONG

UNDER THE SEA, THE BIRDS HAVE SCALES FOR FEATHERS. I KNOW, I KNOW, OH, OH, OH.

SIT WITH ME, CHILD.

GREYSCALE HAD ALMOST CLAIMED THE GIRL IN THE CRIB, LEAVING HER WITH FLESH STIFF AND DEAD, AND STONY TO THE TOUCH.

SHE WAS THE SADDEST CHILD HE KNEW.

THIS IS EARLY TO COME CALLING, SCARCE PAST DAWN. YOU SHOULD BE SNUG IN YOUR BED.

I HAD BAD DREAMS, ABOUT THE DRAGONS. THEY WERE COMING TO EAT ME.

WE HAVE TALKED OF THIS BEFORE. THE DRAGONS CANNOT COME TO LIFE. THEY ARE CARVED OF STONE, CHILD.

IN OLDEN DAYS, OUR ISLAND WAS THE WESTERNMOST OUTPOST OF THE GREAT FREEHOLD OF VALYRIA. IT WAS THE VALYRIANS WHO RAISED THIS CITADEL, AND THEY HAD WAYS OF SHAPING STONE SINCE LOST TO US.

THE VALYRIANS FASHIONED THESE TOWERS IN THE SHAPE OF DRAGONS TO MAKE THEIR FORTRESS SEEM MORE FEARSOME, JUST AS THEY CROWNED THEIR WALLS WITH A THOUSAND GARGOYLES INSTEAD OF SIMPLE CRENELLATIONS.

SO YOU SEE, THERE IS NOTHING TO FEAR.

WHAT ABOUT THE THING IN THE SKY? I HEARD THE RED WOMAN TELL MOTHER THAT IT WAS DRAGONSBREATH.

IF THE DRAGONS ARE BREATHING, DOESN'T THAT MEAN THEY ARE COMING TO LIFE?

THE RED WOMAN. ILL ENOUGH SHE'D FILLED THE MOTHER WITH HER MADNESS. MUST SHE POISON THE DAUGHTER'S DREAMS AS WELL?

THE THING IN THE SKY IS A COMET, SWEET CHILD. A STAR WITH A TAIL, LOST IN THE HEAVENS. IT WILL BE GONE SOON ENOUGH.

MOTHER SAID THE WHITE RAVEN MEANS IT'S NOT SUMMER ANYMORE.

RING-A-LING CLONG

THAT IS SO, MY LADY. THE WHITE RAVENS FLY ONLY FROM THE CITADEL. THEY ARE LARGER THAN OTHER RAVENS, AND MORE CLEVER.

THIS ONE CAME TO TELL US THAT THE CONCLAVE HAS DECLARED THIS GREAT SUMMER DONE AT LAST.

TEN YEARS, TWO TURNS, AND SIXTEEN DAYS IT LASTED, THE LONGEST SUMMER IN LIVING MEMORY.

WILL IT GET COLD NOW?

IN TIME. IF THE GODS ARE GOOD, THEY WILL GRANT US A WARM AUTUMN AND BOUNTIFUL HARVESTS, SO WE MIGHT PREPARE FOR THE WINTER TO COME.

UNDER THE SEA, IT SNOWS UP, AND THE RAIN IS DRY AS BONE. I KNOW, I KNOW, OH, OH, OH.

CLANG-A-LANG CLONG CLONG

WILL IT TRULY SNOW?

IT WILL.

AH, HERE IS PYLOS WITH THE BIRD.

OOH!

HERE.

THIS IS THE LADY SHIREEN.

LADY, LADY.

IT TALKS!

A FEW WORDS. AS I SAID, THEY ARE CLEVER, THESE BIRDS.

CLEVER BIRD, CLEVER MAN, CLEVER CLEVER FOOL.

THE SHADOWS COME TO DANCE, MY LORD, DANCE MY LORD, DANCE MY LORD. THE SHADOWS COME TO STAY, MY LORD, STAY MY LORD, STAY MY LORD.

HE SINGS THAT ALL THE TIME. I TOLD HIM TO STOP BUT HE WON'T.

PATCHFACE HAD COME TO THEM FROM VOLANTIS, ACROSS THE NARROW SEA, BUT HAD GONE DOWN WITH LORD STEFFON BARATHEON AND HIS LADY WIFE WHEN THEIR SHIP HAD FOUNDERED.

HE HAD WASHED UP ON THE BEACH TWO DAYS LATER, STILL ALIVE, YET BROKEN IN BODY AND MIND.

A FOOL SINGS WHAT HE WILL. YOU MUST NOT TAKE HIS WORDS TO HEART.

ON THE MORROW HE MAY REMEMBER ANOTHER SONG, AND THIS ONE WILL NEVER BE HEARD AGAIN.

MAESTER, PARDONS... BUT SER DAVOS RETURNED LAST NIGHT.

HE IS WITH THE KING. THEY HAVE BEEN TOGETHER MOST OF THE NIGHT.

I THOUGHT YOU WOULD WANT TO KNOW AT ONCE.

I SHOULD HAVE BEEN TOLD. I SHOULD HAVE BEEN WOKEN.

PARDONS, MY LADY, BUT I MUST SPEAK WITH YOUR LORD FATHER. PYLOS, GIVE ME YOUR ARM.

THERE ARE TOO MANY STEPS IN THIS CASTLE, AND IT SEEMS TO ME THEY ADD A FEW EVERY NIGHT, JUST TO VEX ME.

WAIT HERE. IT'S BEST I SEE HIM ALONE.

IT IS A LONG CLIMB, MAESTER.

YOU THINK I HAVE FORGOTTEN?

I HAVE CLIMBED THESE STEPS SO OFTEN I KNOW EACH ONE BY NAME.

TWO YEARS PAST, CRESSEN HAD FALLEN AND SHATTERED HIS HIP, AND IT HAD NEVER MENDED PROPERLY.

HE KNEW PYLOS HAD COME TO REPLACE HIM WHEN HE DIED, BUT HE DID NOT MIND.

SOMEONE MUST TAKE HIS PLACE, AND SOONER THAN HE WOULD LIKE...

MAESTER?

AH. SER DAVOS.

WHEN DID YOU RETURN?

IN THE BLACK OF MORNING. MY FAVORITE TIME.

AND?

IT IS AS YOU WARNED HIM. THEY WILL NOT RISE, MAESTER. NOT FOR HIM. THEY DO NOT LOVE HIM.

YOU SPOKE TO THEM ALL?

ALL? NO. ONLY THOSE THAT WOULD SEE ME.

THEY DO NOT LOVE ME EITHER, THESE HIGHBORNS. TO THEM I'LL ALWAYS BE THE ONION KNIGHT.

DURING THE SIEGE OF STORM'S END, WHEN THE GARRISON WAS DOWN TO ROOTS AND RATS, DAVOS THE SMUGGLER HAD DARED THE CORDON ONE DARK NIGHT WITH A HOLD CRAMMED WITH ONIONS AND SALT FISH.

LITTLE ENOUGH, BUT IT HAD KEPT THE GARRISON ALIVE LONG ENOUGH FOR EDDARD STARK TO REACH STORM'S END AND BREAK THE SIEGE.

LORD STANNIS HAD REWARDED DAVOS WITH A KNIGHT'S HONORS...

...BUT HAD TAKEN A JOINT OF EACH FINGER ON DAVOS' LEFT HAND TO PAY FOR ALL HIS YEARS OF SMUGGLING.

WHAT REASONS DID THE LORDS GIVE FOR THEIR REFUSALS?

SOME GAVE ME SOFT WORDS AND SOME BLUNT, BUT IN THE END WORDS ARE JUST WIND.

YOU COULD BRING HIM NO HOPE?

ONLY THE FALSE SORT, AND I'D NOT DO THAT. HE HAD THE TRUTH FROM ME.

TRUTH CAN BE A BITTER DRAUGHT, EVEN FOR A MAN LIKE LORD STANNIS. HE THINKS ONLY OF RETURNING TO KING'S LANDING TO TEAR DOWN HIS ENEMIES AND CLAIM WHAT IS RIGHTFULLY HIS. YET NOW...

IF HE TAKES HIS MEAGER HOST TO KING'S LANDING, IT WILL BE TO DIE. HE DOES NOT HAVE THE NUMBERS. I TOLD HIM AS MUCH, BUT YOU KNOW HIS PRIDE.

MY FINGERS WILL GROW BACK BEFORE THAT MAN BENDS TO SENSE.

YOU HAVE DONE ALL YOU COULD. NOW I MUST ADD MY VOICE TO YOURS.

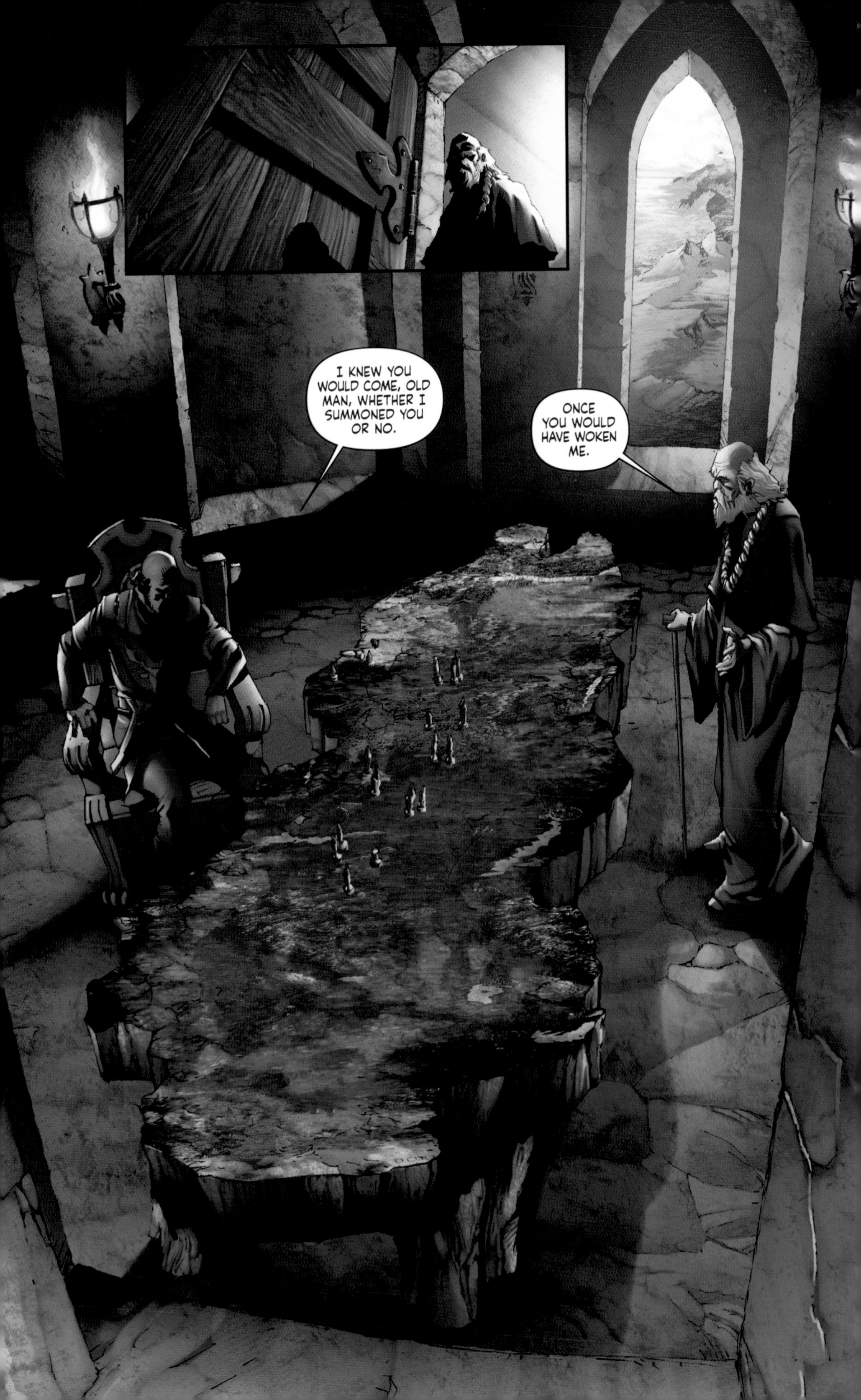
I KNEW YOU WOULD COME, OLD MAN, WHETHER I SUMMONED YOU OR NO.
ONCE YOU WOULD HAVE WOKEN ME.

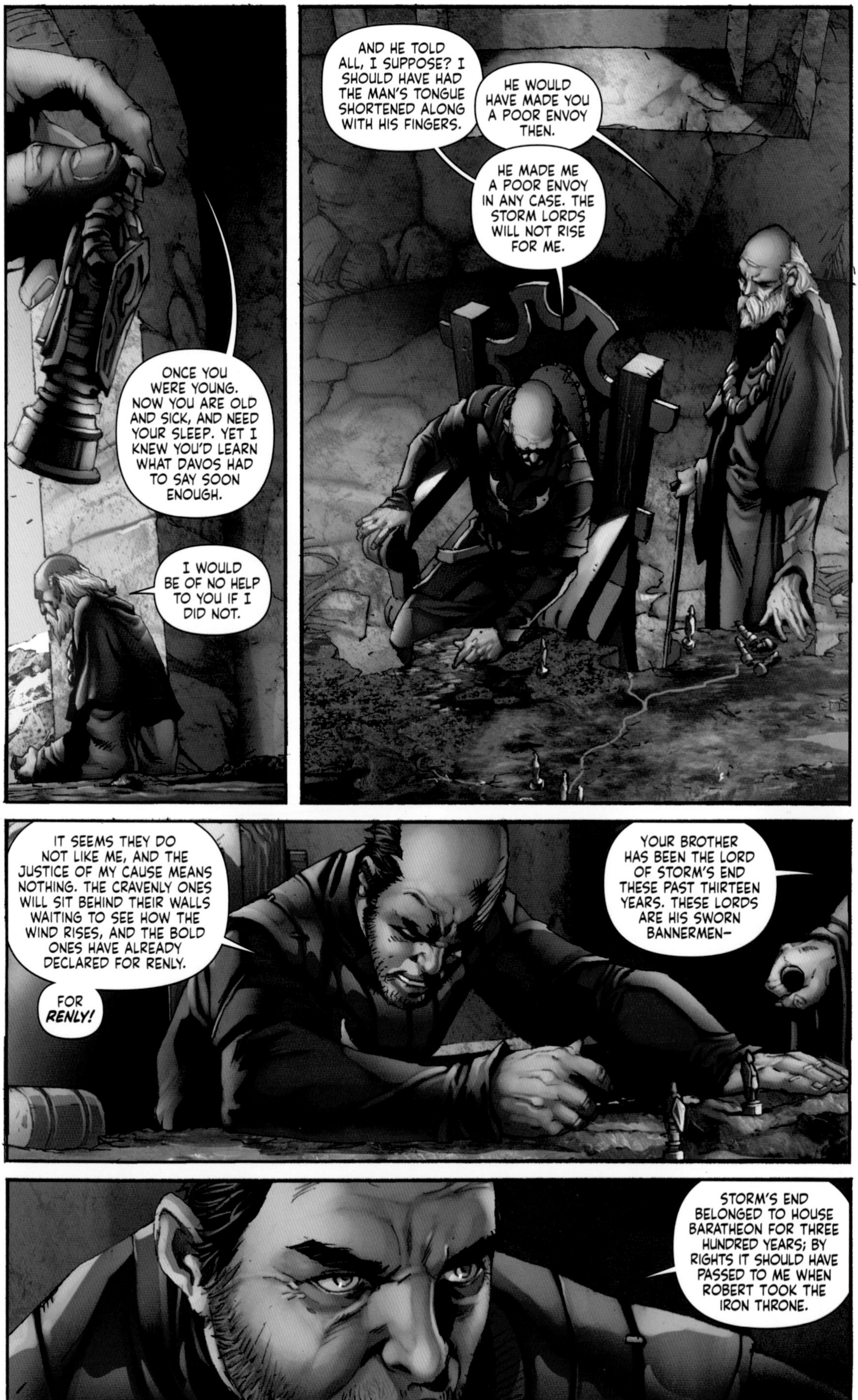
ONCE YOU WERE YOUNG. NOW YOU ARE OLD AND SICK, AND NEED YOUR SLEEP. YET I KNEW YOU'D LEARN WHAT DAVOS HAD TO SAY SOON ENOUGH.
I WOULD BE OF NO HELP TO YOU IF I DID NOT.
AND HE TOLD ALL, I SUPPOSE? I SHOULD HAVE HAD THE MAN'S TONGUE SHORTENED ALONG WITH HIS FINGERS.
HE WOULD HAVE MADE YOU A POOR ENVOY THEN.
HE MADE ME A POOR ENVOY IN ANY CASE. THE STORM LORDS WILL NOT RISE FOR ME.
IT SEEMS THEY DO NOT LIKE ME, AND THE JUSTICE OF MY CAUSE MEANS NOTHING. THE CRAVENLY ONES WILL SIT BEHIND THEIR WALLS WAITING TO SEE HOW THE WIND RISES, AND THE BOLD ONES HAVE ALREADY DECLARED FOR RENLY.
FOR *RENLY!*
YOUR BROTHER HAS BEEN THE LORD OF STORM'S END THESE PAST THIRTEEN YEARS. THESE LORDS ARE HIS SWORN BANNERMEN–
STORM'S END BELONGED TO HOUSE BARATHEON FOR THREE HUNDRED YEARS; BY RIGHTS IT SHOULD HAVE PASSED TO ME WHEN ROBERT TOOK THE IRON THRONE.

YET DRAGONSTONE HAD LONG BEEN THE SEAT OF HOUSE TARGARYEN. ROBERT NEEDED A MAN'S STRENGTH TO RULE HERE, AND RENLY WAS BUT A CHILD.

HE IS A CHILD STILL—A THIEVING CHILD WHO THINKS TO SNATCH THE CROWN OFF MY BROW! WHAT HAS RENLY EVER DONE TO EARN A THRONE?

YOUR TRUE ENEMIES ARE THE LANNISTERS, MY LORD. IF YOU AND YOUR BROTHER WERE TO MAKE COMMON CAUSE AGAINST THEM—

I WILL NOT TREAT WITH RENLY! NOT WHILE HE CALLS HIMSELF A KING.

EDDARD STARK'S SON HAS BEEN PROCLAIMED KING IN THE NORTH, WITH ALL THE POWER OF WINTERFELL AND RIVERRUN BEHIND HIM...

A GREEN BOY, AND ANOTHER FALSE KING. AM I TO ACCEPT A BROKEN REALM?

SURELY HALF A KINGDOM IS BETTER THAN NONE, AND IF YOU HELP THE BOY AVENGE HIS FATHER'S MURDER—

WHY SHOULD I AVENGE EDDARD STARK? THE MAN WAS NOTHING TO ME. OH, ROBERT LOVED HIM, TO BE SURE. LOVED HIM AS A BROTHER, HOW OFTEN DID I HEAR THAT?

I WAS HIS BROTHER, NOT NED STARK, BUT YOU WOULD NEVER HAVE KNOWN IT BY THE WAY HE TREATED ME.

I HELD STORM'S END FOR HIM, WATCHING GOOD MEN STARVE, BUT DID ROBERT THANK ME? NO. HE THANKED STARK, FOR LIFTING THE SIEGE.

INDEED, GREAT WRONGS HAVE BEEN DONE YOU, BUT THE PAST IS DUST. THE FUTURE MAY YET BE WON IF YOU JOIN WITH THE STARKS.

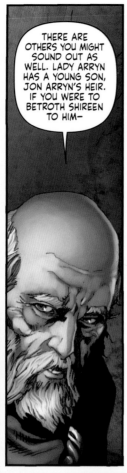

THERE ARE OTHERS YOU MIGHT SOUND OUT AS WELL. LADY ARRYN HAS A YOUNG SON, JON ARRYN'S HEIR. IF YOU WERE TO BETROTH SHIREEN TO HIM—

THE BOY IS WEAK AND SICKLY, AND LYSA WILL NEVER PART WITH HIM. I PROMISE YOU THAT.

THEN SEND SHIREEN TO THE EYRIE. DRAGONSTONE IS A GRIM HOME FOR A CHILD. LET HER FOOL GO WITH HER, SO SHE WILL HAVE A FAMILIAR FACE ABOUT HER...

AND MUST THE RIGHTFUL LORD OF THE SEVEN KINGDOMS BEG FOR HELP FROM WIDOW WOMEN AND USURPERS?

LADY SELYSE...

MY LADY, I DO NOT BEG. OF ANYONE.

I AM PLEASED TO HEAR IT, MY LORD. LADY ARRYN OWES YOU HER ALLEGIANCE, AS DO THE STARKS, YOUR BROTHER RENLY, AND ALL THE REST.

IT WOULD NOT BE FITTING TO PLEAD AND BARGAIN WITH THEM FOR WHAT IS RIGHTFULLY YOURS BY THE GRACE OF GOD.

YOUR GOD CAN KEEP HIS GRACE. IT'S SWORDS I NEED, NOT BLESSINGS.

DO YOU HAVE AN ARMY HIDDEN SOMEWHERE THAT YOU'VE NOT TOLD ME OF?

THERE IS ANOTHER WAY.

LOOK OUT YOUR WINDOWS, MY LORD. THERE IS THE SIGN YOU HAVE WAITED FOR, BLAZONED ON THE SKY.

RED, IT IS, THE RED OF FLAME, RED FOR THE FIERY HEART OF THE TRUE GOD. IT IS HIS BANNER—AND YOURS!

IT MEANS YOUR TIME HAS COME, YOUR GRACE.

YOU ARE MEANT TO SAIL FROM THIS DESOLATE ROCK AS AEGON THE CONQUEROR ONCE SAILED, TO SWEEP ALL BEFORE YOU AS HE DID. ONLY SAY THE WORD, AND EMBRACE THE POWER OF THE LORD OF LIGHT!

AND HOW MANY SWORDS WILL THE LORD OF LIGHT PUT INTO MY HAND?

ALL YOU NEED. THE SWORDS OF STORM'S END AND HIGHGARDEN FOR A START, AND ALL THEIR LORDS BANNERMEN.

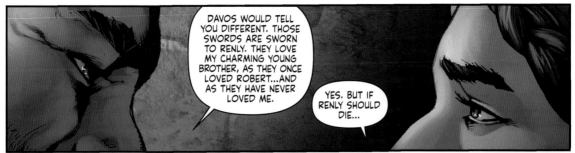

DAVOS WOULD TELL YOU DIFFERENT. THOSE SWORDS ARE SWORN TO RENLY. THEY LOVE MY CHARMING YOUNG BROTHER, AS THEY ONCE LOVED ROBERT...AND AS THEY HAVE NEVER LOVED ME.

YES. BUT IF RENLY SHOULD DIE...

YOUR GRACE, WHATEVER FOLLIES RENLY HAS COMMITTED—

FOLLIES? I CALL THEM TREASONS!

MELISANDRE HAS GAZED INTO THE FLAMES, AND SEEN HIM DEAD.

FRATRICIDE... MY LORD, THIS IS EVIL, UNTHINKABLE...PLEASE, LISTEN TO ME.

AND WHAT WILL YOU TELL HIM, MAESTER? HOW HE MIGHT WIN HALF A KINGDOM IF HE GOES TO THE STARKS ON HIS KNEES AND SELLS OUR DAUGHTER TO LYSA ARRYN?

I HAVE HEARD YOUR COUNSEL, CRESSEN. NOW I WILL HEAR HERS.

YOU ARE DISMISSED.

WHEN A MAESTER DONNED HIS COLLAR, HE PUT ASIDE THE HOPE OF CHILDREN, YET CRESSEN HAD OFT FELT A FATHER NONETHELESS.

ROBERT, STANNIS, RENLY... THREE SONS HE HAD RAISED AFTER THE ANGRY SEA CLAIMED LORD STEFFON.

HAVE I LIVED SO LONG FOR THIS?

HAVE I DONE SO ILL THAT I MUST WATCH ONE KILL THE OTHER?

THE RED WOMAN WAS THE HEART OF IT.

THE RED WOMAN, THE SERVANTS HAD NAMED HER, AFRAID TO SPEAK HER NAME.

I WILL SPEAK HER NAME. MELISANDRE OF ASSHAI. *HER.*

SORCERESS, SHADOWBINDER, AND PRIESTESS OF THE LORD OF LIGHT.

MELISANDRE, WHOSE MADNESS MUST NOT BE ALLOWED TO SPREAD BEYOND DRAGONSTONE.

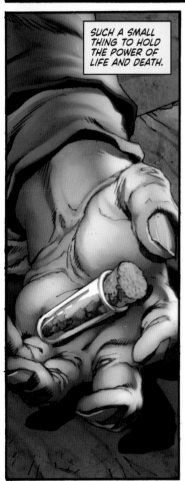

SUCH A SMALL THING TO HOLD THE POWER OF LIFE AND DEATH.

IN THE CITADEL, IT WAS CALLED THE STRANGLER. DISSOLVED IN WINE, IT WOULD MAKE THE MUSCLES IN A MAN'S THROAT CLENCH TIGHTER THAN ANY FIST.

THEY SAID THE VICTIM'S FACE TURNED AS PURPLE AS THE LITTLE CRYSTAL SEED FROM WHICH HIS DEATH WAS GROWN...

AND THIS VERY NIGHT LORD STANNIS WOULD FEAST HIS BANNERMEN, HIS LADY WIFE SELYSE...AND THE RED WOMAN, MELISANDRE OF ASSHAI.

PERHAPS IT IS MY COMET... AN OMEN OF BLOOD...

"...FORETELLING MURDER."

LORD STANNIS...

MY LORD, IT IS VITAL THAT YOU MAKE COMMON CAUSE WITH LORD STARK AND LADY ARRYN...

I MAKE COMMON CAUSE WITH NO ONE.

NO MORE THAN LIGHT MAKES COMMON CAUSE WITH DARKNESS.

KING STANNIS.

YOU FORGET YOURSELF, MAESTER.

HE IS OLD AND HIS MIND WANDERS. WHAT IS IT, CRESSEN? SPEAK.

THE STARKS SEEK TO STEAL HALF MY KINGDOM, EVEN AS THE LANNISTERS HAVE STOLEN MY THRONE AND MY OWN SWEET BROTHER THE SWORDS THAT ARE MINE BY RIGHTS.

THEY ARE ALL USURPERS, AND THEY ARE ALL MY ENEMIES!

YOU CANNOT HOPE TO TRIUMPH WITHOUT ALLIES.

HE *HAS* AN ALLY. R'HLLOR, THE LORD OF LIGHT, THE HEART OF FIRE, THE GOD OF FLAME AND SHADOW.

GODS MAKE UNCERTAIN ALLIES AT BEST...AND THAT ONE HAS NO POWER HERE.

YOU THINK NOT?

I...

MAYHAPS I HAVE BEEN... A FOOL.

YOU ARE TOO ILL AND TOO CONFUSED TO BE OF USE TO ME, OLD MAN.

PYLOS WILL COUNSEL ME HENCEFORTH. I WILL NOT HAVE YOU KILL YOURSELF IN MY SERVICE.

LADY MELISANDRE. WILL YOU SHARE A CUP OF WINE? IN HONOR OF YOUR LORD OF LIGHT? A TOAST TO HIS POWER?

AS YOU WILL.

AND NOW YOU.

HIS HANDS WERE SHAKING, BUT HE MADE HIMSELF BE STRONG.

A MAESTER OF THE CITADEL MUST NOT BE AFRAID.

HE *DOES* HAVE POWER HERE, MY LORD.

AND FIRE?

FIRE CLEANSES.

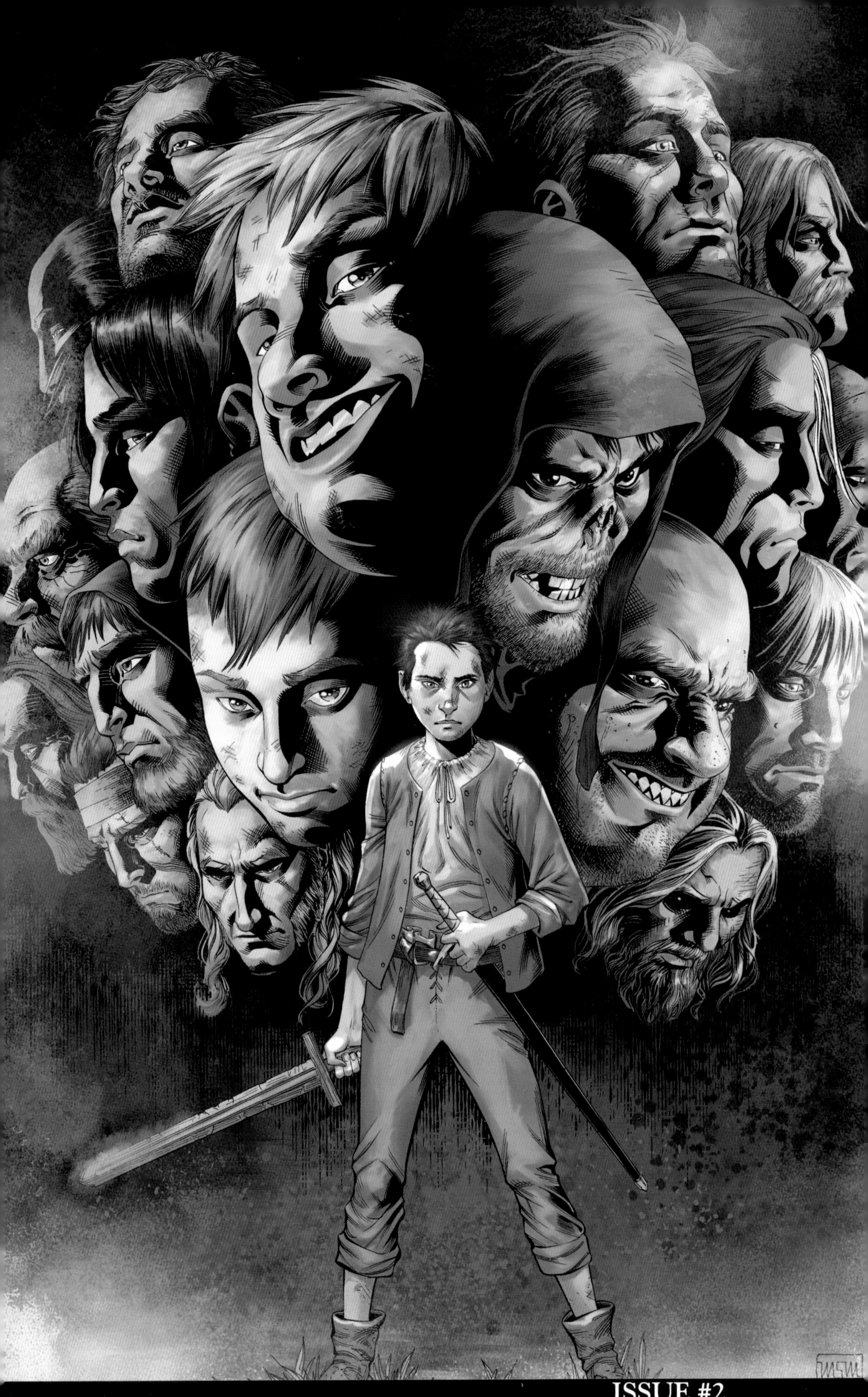

ISSUE #2

ARYA

WHEN YOREN HAD DRAGGED HER INTO THAT ALLEY, ARYA HAD THOUGHT HE MEANT TO KILL HER.

I'M TAKING MEN AND BOYS FROM THE CITY.

NOW YOU HOLD STILL, "BOY."

LORD EDDARD GAVE ME PICK O' THE DUNGEONS, AND I DIDN'T FIND NO LITTLE LORDLINGS DOWN THERE.

FROM NOW ON YOU'RE ARRY, AN ORPHAN BOY.

GATE SHOULDN'T BE HARD, BUT THE ROAD'S ANOTHER MATTER. YOU GOT A LONG WAY TO GO IN BAD COMPANY.

SO YOU KEEP TO YOURSELF AND MAKE YOUR WATER IN THE WOODS, ALONE.

THAT'LL BE THE HARDEST PART, THE PISSING.

LEAVING KING'S LANDING WAS EASY, JUST LIKE YOREN HAD SAID.

THE LANNISTER GUARDSMEN ON THE GATE WERE STOPPING EVERYONE, BUT YOREN CALLED ONE BY NAME AND THEIR WAGONS WERE WAVED THROUGH.

NO ONE SPARED ARYA A GLANCE. THEY WERE LOOKING FOR A HIGHBORN GIRL, NOT A BOY WITH HIS HAIR CHOPPED OFF.

YOREN WAS WRONG ABOUT THE PISSING, THOUGH; THAT WASN'T THE HARDEST PART.

LOMMY GREENHANDS AND HOT PIE WERE THE HARDEST.

ORPHAN BOYS YOREN HAD PLUCKED FROM THE STREETS.

LOMMY HAD BEEN A DYER'S APPRENTICE BEFORE HE WAS CAUGHT STEALING.

HOT PIE'S MOTHER HAD BEEN A BAKER, AND HE'D PUSHED HER CART THROUGH THE STREETS ALL DAY, SHOUTING "HOT PIES! HOT PIES!".

AT WINTERFELL THEY CALLED HER "ARYA HORSEFACE" AND SHE THOUGHT NOTHING COULD BE WORSE.

BUT THAT WAS BEFORE LOMMY HAD NAMED HER "LUMPYHEAD."

LOOK AT THAT SWORD LUMPYHEAD'S GOT. WHERE'S A GUTTER RAT LIKE LUMPYHEAD GET HIM A SWORD?

MAYBE HE'S A LITTLE SQUIRE. SOME LORDY LORD'S LITTLE SQUIRE BOY.

HE AIN'T NO SQUIRE, LOOK AT HIM. I BET THAT'S NOT EVEN A REAL SWORD. I BET IT'S MADE OF TIN.

IT'S CASTLE-FORGED STEEL, AND YOU BETTER SHUT YOUR MOUTH!

WHERE'D YOU GET A BLADE LIKE THAT, LUMPYFACE?

LUMPY*HEAD*. HE PROB'LY STOLE IT.

I DID NOT!

GO ON, TAKE IT OFF HIM, I DARE YOU.

LUMPYFACE, YOU GIMME THAT SWORD! YOU DON'T KNOW HOW TO USE IT.

"YES, I DO," ARYA THOUGHT, AS SHE SLID HER WOODEN PRACTICE SWORD FROM HER BELT.

YOU CAN HAVE THIS ONE INSTEAD.

HEY...

CRAAACK

"I KILLED A BOY, A FAT BOY LIKE YOU."

THWACK

"AND I'LL KILL YOU TOO, IF YOU DON'T LEAVE ME ALONE..."

WHACK

STOP IT, STOP IT, STOP IT!

ENOUGH! YOU WANT TO KILL THE FOOL?

ANY MORE OF THIS, I'LL TIE YOU LOT BEHIND THE WAGONS AND *DRAG* YOU TO THE WALL!

YOREN HAD TAKEN GROWN MEN FROM THE DUNGEONS AS WELL, BUT THE WORST WERE THE THREE HE FOUND IN THE BLACK CELLS.

YOU COME WITH ME, BOY. *NOW.*

THEY MUST HAVE SCARED EVEN HIM, BECAUSE HE KEPT THEM CHAINED HAND AND FOOT.

THE FAT ONE SNAPPED HIS POINTY TEETH AND HISSED AS THEY PASSED, BUT ARYA IGNORED HIM.

NEXT TIME YOU TAKE THAT STICK TO ONE OF YOUR BROTHERS, YOU'LL GET TWICE WHAT YOU GIVE, YOU HEAR ME?

"CALM AS STILL WATER," ARYA TOLD HERSELF, THE WAY SYRIO FOREL HAD TAUGHT HER. *"AND THEY'RE NOT MY BROTHERS!"*

WHACK

THAT PIE BOY... IT WASN'T HIM AS KILLED YOUR FATHER, GIRL, NOR THAT THIEVING LOMMY NEITHER. HITTING THEM WON'T BRING HIM BACK.

THWACK

I KNOW.

HERE'S SOMETHING YOU DON'T KNOW. IT WASN'T SUPPOSED TO HAPPEN LIKE THIS.

I WAS SET TO LEAVE, WAGONS BOUGHT AND LOADED, AND A MAN COMES WITH A BOY FOR ME, AND A PURSE OF COIN, AND A MESSAGE.

LORD EDDARD'S TO TAKE THE BLACK, HE SAYS TO ME, HE'LL BE GOING WITH YOU. WHY D'YOU THINK I WAS THERE? ONLY SOMETHING WENT QUEER.

JOFFREY. SOMEONE SHOULD KILL HIM!

SOMEONE WILL, BUT IT WON'T BE ME. NOR YOU NEITHER.

GOT SOURLEAF BACK AT THE WAGONS. YOU'LL CHEW SOME.

IT'LL HELP WITH THE STING.

THAT NIGHT, SHE STARED UP AT THE GREAT RED COMET.

YOREN HAD MADE HER LOOK AWAY WHEN HER FATHER WAS BEHEADED WITH HIS OWN GREATSWORD, ICE, BUT IT SEEMED TO HER THE COMET LOOKED LIKE ICE MUST HAVE, AFTER.

AND WHEN AT LAST SHE SLEPT, SHE DREAMED OF HOME.

BRAN

OF LATE, BRAN OFTEN DREAMED OF WOLVES.

THEY ARE TALKING TO ME, BROTHER TO BROTHER...

HE COULD ALMOST UNDERSTAND RICKON'S SHAGGYDOG AND HIS OWN SUMMER...AS IF THEY WERE SINGING IN A LANGUAGE HE HAD ONCE KNOWN AND SOMEHOW FORGOTTEN.

"IT'S FREEDOM THEY'RE CALLING FOR," DECLARED FARLEN THE KENNELMASTER. "WILD THINGS BELONG IN THE WILD, NOT IN A CASTLE."

OOOOOOOOOOOOOOOOOOO-OOOOOOO AHOOOOOOOOOOOOOOOO

"THEY WANT TO HUNT," SAID GAGE THE COOK. "A WOLF SMELLS BETTER'N ANY MAN. LIKE AS NOT, THEY'VE CAUGHT THE SCENT O' PREY."

OOOOOOOOOOOOOOOOOOO-OOOOOO AHOOOOOOOOOOOOOOOO

"WOLVES OFTEN HOWL AT THE MOON," MAESTER LUWIN TOLD HIM. "SEE HOW BRIGHT THE COMET IS, BRAN? PERCHANCE SUMMER AND SHAGGYDOG THINK IT IS THE MOON."

OOOOOOOOOOOOOOOOO-OOOOO AHOOOOOOOOOOOOOOO

"YOUR WOLVES HAVE MORE WIT THAN YOUR MAESTER," OSHA SAID. "THEY KNOW TRUTHS THE GREY MAN HAS FORGOTTEN. BLOOD AND FIRE, BOY, AND NOTHING SWEET."

OOOOOOOOOOOOOOOOOO-OOOOOO AHOOOOOOOOOOOOOOO

"DRAGONS," WAS ALL OLD NAN SAID, LIFTING HER HEAD AND SNIFFING. "IT BE DRAGONS, BOY."

OOOO...

AND STILL THE DIREWOLVES HOWLED.

OOOOOOO OOOOOOO-OOOOO, AHOOOOOOOOOO OOOO!

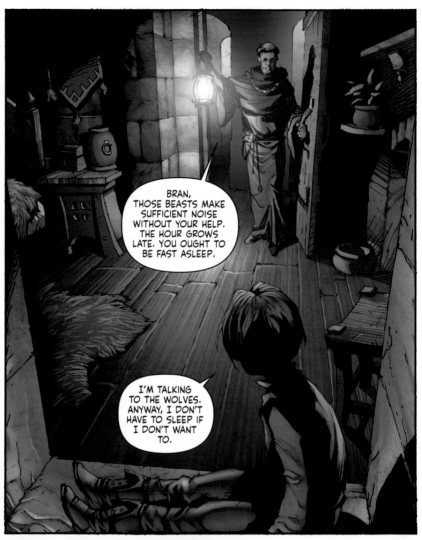

BRAN, THOSE BEASTS MAKE SUFFICIENT NOISE WITHOUT YOUR HELP. THE HOUR GROWS LATE. YOU OUGHT TO BE FAST ASLEEP.

I'M TALKING TO THE WOLVES. ANYWAY, I DON'T HAVE TO SLEEP IF I DON'T WANT TO.

ALL MEN MUST SLEEP, BRAN. EVEN PRINCES.

WHEN I SLEEP I TURN INTO A WOLF. DO WOLVES DREAM?

ALL CREATURES DREAM, I THINK, YET NOT AS MEN DO.

DO TREES DREAM?

TREES? NO...

THEY DO. THEY DREAM TREE DREAMS.

I DREAM OF A TREE SOMETIMES. A WEIRWOOD, LIKE THE ONE IN THE GODSWOOD. IT CALLS TO ME.

THE WOLF DREAMS ARE BETTER. I SMELL THINGS, AND SOMETIMES I CAN TASTE THE BLOOD.

IF YOU WOULD ONLY SPEND MORE TIME WITH THE OTHER CHILDREN...

I HATE THE OTHER CHILDREN!

I COMMANDED YOU TO SEND THEM AWAY.

THE FREYS ARE YOUR LADY MOTHER'S WARDS, SENT HERE TO BE FOSTERED AT HER EXPRESS COMMAND.

IT IS NOT FOR YOU TO EXPEL THEM.

WHEN THE BOYS HAD ARRIVED FROM THE TWINS, IT HAD BEEN RICKON WHO WANTED THEM GONE.

HE HAD SCREAMED THAT HE WANTED MOTHER AND FATHER AND ROBB, NOT THESE STRANGERS.

BOTH OF THEM WERE CALLED WALDER FREY AFTER THEIR GRANDFATHER, BUT WERE KNOWN AS BIG AND LITTLE WALDER.

I'M LITTLE WALDER. HE'S FIFTY-TWO DAYS OLDER THAN ME, SO HE WAS BIGGER AT FIRST, BUT I GREW FASTER.

I'M BIG WALDER, AND WE'RE NOT THE ONLY WALDERS EITHER. THERE'S EVEN GIRLS NAMED WALDA.

WE HAVE OUR OWN NAMES AT WINTERFELL.

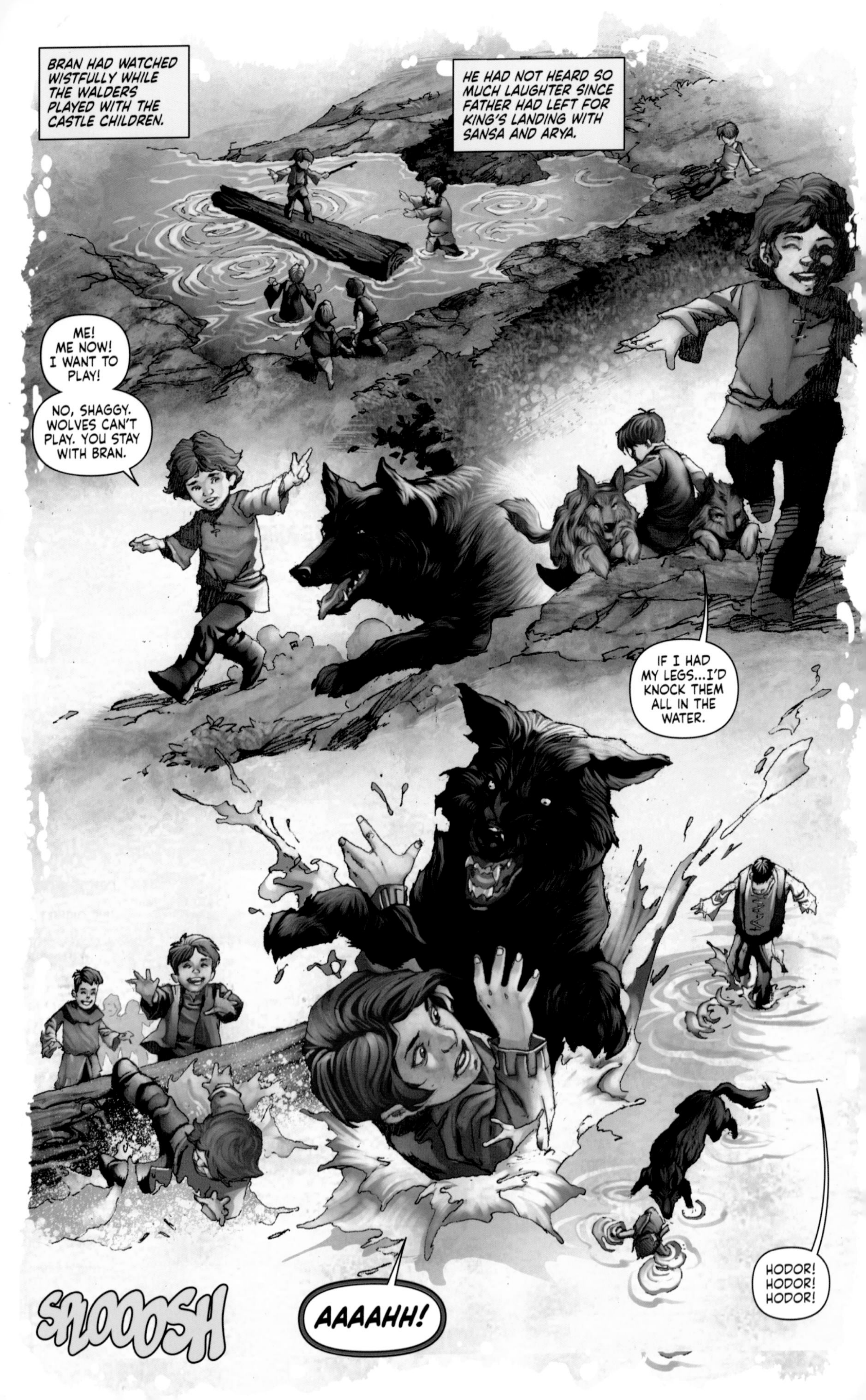
BRAN HAD WATCHED WISTFULLY WHILE THE WALDERS PLAYED WITH THE CASTLE CHILDREN.
HE HAD NOT HEARD SO MUCH LAUGHTER SINCE FATHER HAD LEFT FOR KING'S LANDING WITH SANSA AND ARYA.
ME! ME NOW! I WANT TO PLAY!
NO, SHAGGY. WOLVES CAN'T PLAY. YOU STAY WITH BRAN.
IF I HAD MY LEGS...I'D KNOCK THEM ALL IN THE WATER.
SPLOOOSH
AAAAHH!
HODOR! HODOR! HODOR!

AFTER THAT, RICKON DECIDED HE **LIKED** THE WALDERS. WITH RICKON BY THEIR SIDE, THE WALDERS PLUNDERED THE KITCHENS, RACED ROUND THE WALLS, AND TRAINED WITH WOODEN SWORDS UNDER SER RODRIK'S SHARP EYE.

I'VE MADE YOU A SLEEPING DRAUGHT, BRAN.

THIS WILL GIVE YOU DREAMLESS SLEEP. SWEET, DREAMLESS SLEEP.

IT WILL?

YES. DRINK.

COME THE MORN, YOU'LL FEEL BETTER.

IS IT THE WOLF DREAMS AGAIN?

YOU SHOULD NOT FIGHT SO HARD, BOY. I SEE YOU TALKING TO THE HEART TREE. MIGHT BE THE GODS ARE TRYING TO TALK BACK.

THE GODS?

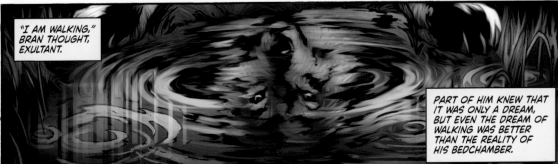

"I AM WALKING," BRAN THOUGHT, EXULTANT.

PART OF HIM KNEW THAT IT WAS ONLY A DREAM, BUT EVEN THE DREAM OF WALKING WAS BETTER THAN THE REALITY OF HIS BEDCHAMBER.

THE COMET LIT HIS WAY, AND HIS FEET WERE SURE.

THE SMELLS FILLED HIS HEAD, ALIVE AND INTOXICATING.

HE WAS MOVING ON FOUR GOOD LEGS, STRONG AND SWIFT, AND HE COULD FEEL THE GROUND UNDERFOOT, THE SOFT CRACKLING OF FALLEN LEAVES.

OOOOOOO-OOOOO

AHOOOOOO

THE TRUE WORLD WAS CALLING, AND HE KNEW HE MUST ANSWER OR DIE.

SANSA

THE MORNING OF KING JOFFREY'S NAME DAY DAWNED BRIGHT AND WINDY.

SANSA WAS WATCHING THE COMET FROM HER WINDOW WHEN SER ARYS OAKHEART ARRIVED TO ESCORT HER TO THE TOURNEY GROUNDS.

WHAT DO YOU THINK IT MEANS?

GLORY TO YOUR BETROTHED, AS IF THE GODS THEMSELVES HAD RAISED A BANNER IN HIS HONOR.

THE SMALLFOLK HAVE NAMED IT KING JOFFREY'S COMET.

DOUBTLESS THAT WAS WHAT THEY TOLD JOFFREY; SANSA WAS NOT SO SURE.

YOU LOOK VERY LOVELY TODAY, MY LADY.

THANK YOU, SER ARYS.

KNOWING JOFFREY WOULD REQUIRE HER TO ATTEND THE TOURNEY, SANSA HAD TAKEN SPECIAL CARE.

THE GOWN HAD LONG SLEEVES TO HIDE THE BRUISES ON HER ARMS.

SHALL WE GO?

IF SHE MUST HAVE ONE OF THE KINGSGUARD DOGGING HER STEPS, SANSA PREFERRED THAT IT BE HIM. HE WAS COURTEOUS, AND WOULD TALK TO HER CORDIALLY.

ONCE HE EVEN OBJECTED WHEN JOFFREY COMMANDED HIM TO HIT HER.

HE **DID** HIT HER IN THE END, BUT NOT AS HARD AS THE OTHERS MIGHT HAVE, AND AT LEAST HE HAD ARGUED.

WHO DO YOU THINK WILL WIN THE DAY'S HONORS?

THE OTHERS OBEYED WITHOUT QUESTION...EXCEPT FOR THE HOUND.

BUT JOFF NEVER ASKED THE HOUND TO PUNISH HER.

HE USED THE OTHER FIVE FOR THAT.

SIT. HAVE YOU HEARD? THE BEGGAR KING IS DEAD.

WHO?

VISERYS. THE LAST SON OF MAD KING AERYS. MOTHER SAYS THE DOTHRAKI FINALLY CROWNED HIM. WITH MOLTEN GOLD.

THAT'S FUNNY, DON'T YOU THINK? THE DRAGON WAS THEIR SIGIL. IT'S ALMOST AS GOOD AS IF SOME WOLF KILLED YOUR TRAITOR BROTHER.

MAYBE I'LL FEED HIM TO WOLVES AFTER I'VE CAUGHT HIM. DID I TELL YOU, I INTEND TO CHALLENGE HIM TO SINGLE COMBAT?

I SHOULD LIKE TO SEE THAT, YOUR GRACE. WILL YOU ENTER THE LISTS TODAY?

MY LADY MOTHER SAID IT WAS NOT FITTING, SINCE THE TOURNEY IS IN MY HONOR. OTHERWISE I WOULD HAVE BEEN CHAMPION. ISN'T THAT SO, DOG?

AGAINST THIS LOT? WHY NOT? THIS IS A TOURNAMENT OF GNATS.

SER MERYN TRANT OF THE KINGSGUARD.

SER HOBBER OF HOUSE REDWYNE, OF THE ARBOR.

THE REDWYNE TWINS WERE THE QUEEN'S UNWILLING GUESTS, EVEN AS SANSA WAS.

SHE WONDERED WHOSE NOTION IT HAD BEEN FOR THEM TO RIDE IN THE TOURNEY. NOT THEIR OWN, SHE THOUGHT.

THIS IS A FEEBLE SHOW.

I WARNED YOU. GNATS.

LOTHOR BRUNE, FREERIDER IN THE SERVICE OF LORD BAELISH.

SER DONTOS THE RED, OF HOUSE HOLLARD.

≋HHH≋ ≋UFF≋

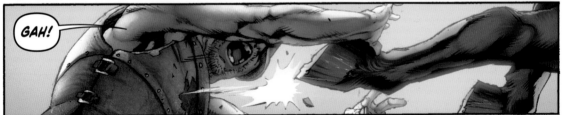

GAH!

I LOSE. FETCH ME SOME MORE WINE.

A CASK FROM THE CELLARS! I'LL SEE HIM DROWNED IN IT.

NO, YOU CAN'T!

WHAT DID YOU SAY?

DID YOU SAY *I CAN'T?*

PLEASE, I ONLY MEANT...IT WOULD BE ILL LUCK, YOUR GRACE...TO, TO KILL A MAN ON YOUR NAME DAY.

THE SINGERS ALL SAY SO...

THE GIRL SPEAKS TRULY. WHAT A MAN SOWS ON HIS NAME DAY, HE REAPS THROUGHOUT THE YEAR.

COULD IT BE *TRUE?* IT WAS JUST SOMETHING SHE'D SAID TO AVOID PUNISHMENT.

TAKE HIM AWAY. I'LL HAVE HIM KILLED ON THE MORROW, THE FOOL.

YES, A FOOL. YOU'RE SO CLEVER, TO SEE IT! YOU OUGHT TO DRESS HIM IN MOTLEY AND MAKE HIM CLOWN FOR YOU.

HE DOESN'T DESERVE THE MERCY OF A QUICK DEATH.

HUH...PERHAPS YOU'RE NOT SO STUPID AS MOTHER SAYS.

YOUR GRACE, SHALL I SUMMON A NEW CHALLENGER FOR BRUNE, OR PROCEED WITH THE NEXT TILT?

NEITHER. THESE ARE GNATS, NOT KNIGHTS. I'D HAVE THEM ALL PUT TO DEATH, ONLY IT'S MY NAME DAY.

THE TOURNEY IS DONE. GET THEM ALL OUT OF MY SIGHT!

THOOM

WHAT?

WHO TOLD THEM TO OPEN THE GATE?

YOUR GRACE.

YOU.

ME.

ALTHOUGH A MORE COURTEOUS GREETING MIGHT BE IN ORDER, FOR AN UNCLE AND AN ELDER.

THEY SAID YOU WERE DEAD.

I WAS SPEAKING TO THE KING, NOT TO HIS CUR.

MY LADY, I AM SORRY FOR YOUR LOSSES. TRULY, THE GODS ARE CRUEL.

SANSA COULDN'T THINK OF A WORD TO SAY. WAS HE MOCKING HER? IT WASN'T THE GODS WHO'D BEEN CRUEL, BUT JOFFREY.

I AM SORRY FOR YOUR LOSS AS WELL, JOFFREY.

WHAT LOSS?

YOUR ROYAL FATHER? A LARGE FIERCE MAN WITH A BLACK BEARD; YOU'LL RECALL HIM IF YOU TRY. HE WAS KING BEFORE YOU.

OH, HIM. YES, IT WAS VERY SAD, A BOAR KILLED HIM.

IS THAT WHAT *"THEY"* SAY, YOUR GRACE?

I'M SORRY MY LADY MOTHER TOOK YOU CAPTIVE, MY LORD.

A GREAT MANY PEOPLE ARE SORRY FOR THAT. AND BEFORE I AM DONE, SOME MAY BE A DEAL SORRIER...

JOFFREY, WHERE MIGHT I FIND YOUR MOTHER?

SHE'S WITH MY COUNCIL. YOUR BROTHER JAIME KEEPS LOSING BATTLES.

HE'S BEEN TAKEN BY THE STARKS AND WE'VE LOST RIVERRUN AND NOW *HER* STUPID BROTHER IS CALLING HIMSELF A KING.

ALL SORTS OF PEOPLE ARE CALLING THEMSELVES KINGS THESE DAYS.

YES. WELL. I'M PLEASED YOU'RE NOT DEAD.

DID YOU BRING ME A PRESENT ON MY NAME DAY?

I DID. MY WITS.

I'D SOONER HAVE ROBB STARK'S HEAD.

TOMMEN, MYRCELLA, COME.

I'D GUARD THAT TONGUE OF YOURS, LITTLE MAN.

IS IT GRIEF FOR YOUR LORD FATHER THAT MAKES YOU SO SAD?

MY...FATHER WAS A TRAITOR. AND MY BROTHER AND LADY MOTHER ARE TRAITORS AS WELL. I AM LOYAL TO MY BELOVED JOFFREY.

NO DOUBT. AS LOYAL AS A DEER SURROUNDED BY WOLVES.

NO...

LIONS.

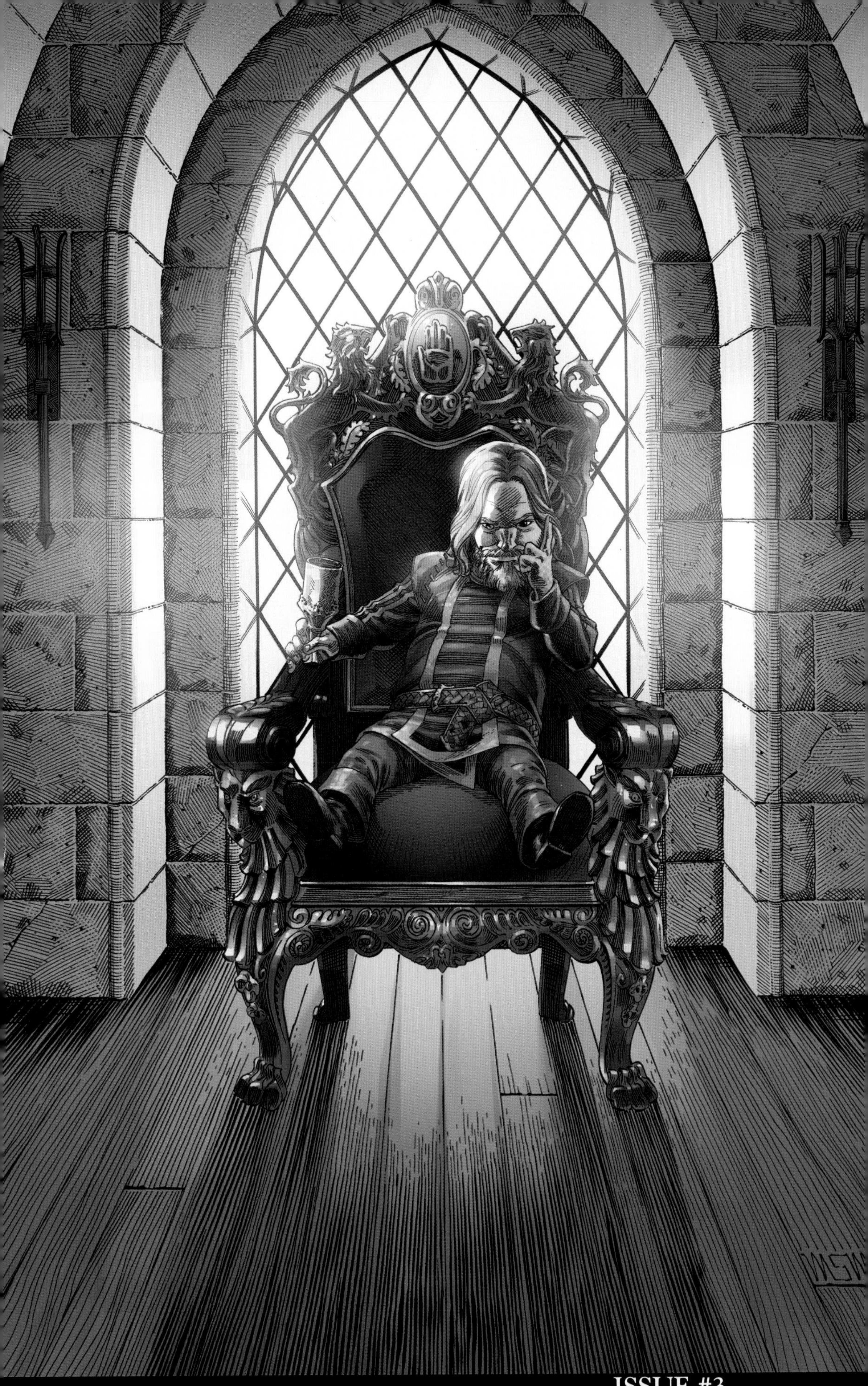

ISSUE #3

JON

HAVE I?

MAESTER AEMON SENT ME TO FIND MAPS FOR THE LORD COMMANDER. I NEVER THOUGHT...

SAM? HAVE YOU BEEN HERE ALL NIGHT?

JON, THE BOOKS, HAVE YOU EVER SEEN THEIR LIKE? THERE ARE THOUSANDS!

DID YOU FIND THE MAPS?

OH, YES. A DOZEN, AT THE LEAST.

THE PAINT HAS FADED, BUT YOU CAN SEE WHERE THE MAPMAKER MARKED THE SITES OF WILDLING VILLAGES.

THERE'S MORE MAPS. IF I HAD TIME TO SEARCH... EVERYTHING'S A JUMBLE.

I COULD SET IT ALL TO ORDER, BUT IT WOULD TAKE YEARS!

THIS VAULT IS A TREASURE, JON. I FOUND WORKS THAT EVEN THE CITADEL DOESN'T HAVE! SCROLLS FROM OLD VALYRIA, COUNTS OF THE SEASONS WRITTEN BY MAESTERS DEAD A THOUSAND YEARS...

THE BOOKS WILL STILL BE HERE WHEN WE RETURN.

IF WE RETURN...

THE OLD BEAR IS TAKING TWO HUNDRED SEASONED MEN. QHORIN HALFHAND WILL BE BRINGING ANOTHER HUNDRED FROM THE SHADOW TOWER.

YOU'LL BE AS SAFE AS IF YOU WERE BACK IN YOUR LORD FATHER'S CASTLE AT HORN HILL.

I WAS NEVER VERY SAFE IN MY FATHER'S CASTLE EITHER.

WE NEED YOU FOR THE RAVENS, SAM. AND SOMEONE HAS TO HELP ME KEEP GRENN HUMBLE.

YOU COULD CARE FOR THE RAVENS, OR GRENN, OR ANYONE! I COULD SHOW YOU HOW...

I'M THE OLD BEAR'S STEWARD. I WON'T HAVE TIME TO WATCH OVER BIRDS AS WELL. SAM, YOU'RE A BROTHER OF THE NIGHT'S WATCH NOW.

A BROTHER OF THE NIGHT'S WATCH SHOULDN'T BE SO SCARED.

WE'RE ALL SCARED. WE'D BE FOOLS IF WE WEREN'T.

MY FATHER TOLD ME, WHAT MATTERS IS HOW WE FACE IT. COME, LORD MORMONT AWAITS US.

THE COMET'S SO BRIGHT YOU CAN SEE IT BY DAY NOW.

NEVER MIND ABOUT COMETS. IT'S MAPS THE OLD BEAR WANTS.

OUTSIDE THE ARMORY, SER ENDREW TARTH WAS WORKING WITH SOME RAW RECRUITS WHO'D COME IN LAST NIGHT.

WHAT DO YOU MAKE OF THEM, SNOW?

THE ARMORER WAS A WELCOME SIGHT. DONAL NOYE HAD PROVED HIMSELF A GOOD FRIEND.

THEY SMELL OF SUMMER.

WITH SUCH DO WE DEFEND THE REALMS OF MEN. YOU'VE HEARD THE TIDINGS OF YOUR BROTHER?

LAST NIGHT. ROBB WILL MAKE A GOOD KING.

I HOPE THAT'S SO, BOY. ONCE I MIGHT HAVE SAID THE SAME OF ROBERT.

THEY SAY YOU FORGED HIS WARHAMMER...

AYE, I WAS SMITH AND ARMORER AT STORM'S END UNTIL I LOST THE ARM.

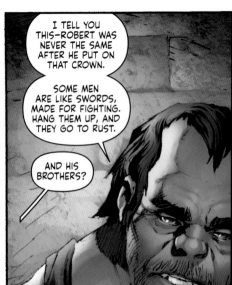

I TELL YOU THIS—ROBERT WAS NEVER THE SAME AFTER HE PUT ON THAT CROWN.

SOME MEN ARE LIKE SWORDS, MADE FOR FIGHTING. HANG THEM UP, AND THEY GO TO RUST.

AND HIS BROTHERS?

"ROBERT WAS THE TRUE STEEL.

"STANNIS IS PURE IRON—BLACK AND HARD AND STRONG, YES, BUT BRITTLE. HE'LL BREAK BEFORE HE BENDS.

"AND RENLY? HE'S COPPER. BRIGHT AND SHINY, PRETTY TO LOOK AT, BUT NOT WORTH ALL THAT MUCH AT THE END OF THE DAY."

"AND WHAT METAL IS ROBB?" JON DID NOT ASK.

MAY THE GODS GO WITH YOU ON THE MORROW, SNOW. YOU BRING BACK THAT UNCLE OF YOURS, YOU HEAR?

WE WILL.

SNOW!

TOOK YOU LONG ENOUGH WITH THOSE MAPS.

WAS THIS ALL YOU COULD FIND? THESE ARE OLD.

OLD, OLD!

THE VILLAGES MAY COME AND GO, BUT THE HILLS AND RIVERS WILL BE IN THE SAME PLACES.

TRUE ENOUGH. HAVE YOU CHOSEN YOUR RAVENS YET, TARLY?

M-M-MAESTER AEMON M-MEANS TO P-PICK THEM COME EVEN-FALL, AFTER THE F-F-FEEDING.

I'LL HAVE HIS BEST. SMART BIRDS, AND STRONG.

STRONG. STRONG STRONG.

IF IT HAPPENS THAT WE'RE ALL BUTCHERED OUT THERE, I MEAN FOR MY SUCCESSOR TO KNOW WHERE AND HOW WE DIED.

TARLY, WHEN I WAS HALF YOUR AGE, MY LADY MOTHER TOLD ME THAT IF I STOOD ABOUT WITH MY MOUTH OPEN, A WEASEL WAS LIKE TO MISTAKE IT FOR HIS LAIR AND RUN DOWN MY THROAT.

IF YOU HAVE SOMETHING TO SAY, SAY IT. OTHERWISE, BEWARE OF WEASELS.

IS THAT BOY AS BIG A FOOL AS HE SEEMS?

FOOL.

HIS LORD FATHER STANDS HIGH IN KING RENLY'S COUNCILS, AND I HAD HALF A NOTION TO DISPATCH HIM... NO, BEST NOT. RENLY IS NOT LIKE TO HEED A QUAKING FAT BOY.

IF IT PLEASE MY LORD, WHAT WOULD YOU HAVE OF KING RENLY?

THE SAME THINGS I'D HAVE OF ALL OF THEM, LAD. MEN, HORSES, SWORDS, ARMOR, GRAIN, CHEESE, WINE, WOOL, NAILS...

THE NIGHT'S WATCH IS NOT PROUD, WE TAKE WHAT IS OFFERED.

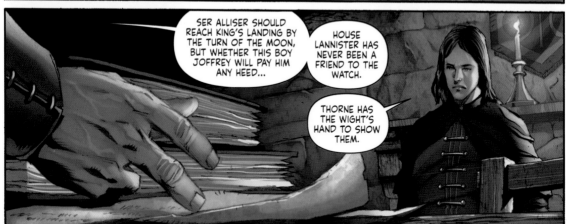

SER ALLISER SHOULD REACH KING'S LANDING BY THE TURN OF THE MOON, BUT WHETHER THIS BOY JOFFREY WILL PAY HIM ANY HEED...

HOUSE LANNISTER HAS NEVER BEEN A FRIEND TO THE WATCH.

THORNE HAS THE WIGHT'S HAND TO SHOW THEM.

SPEAKING OF HANDS. HOW IS YOURS? YOU CAN WIELD LONGCLAW DESPITE THE PAIN?

WELL ENOUGH. I'M TO WORK THE FINGERS EVERY DAY TO KEEP THEM NIMBLE, AS MAESTER AEMON SAID.

BLIND HE MAY BE, BUT AEMON KNOWS WHAT HE'S ABOUT. DO YOU KNOW THAT HE MIGHT HAVE BEEN KING?

HE TOLD ME HIS FATHER WAS KING, BUT NOT...I THOUGHT HIM PERHAPS A YOUNGER SON.

SO HE WAS. HIS FATHER'S FATHER WAS DAERON TARGARYEN, THE SECOND OF HIS NAME, WHO BROUGHT DORNE INTO THE REALM.

AEMON'S FATHER MAEKAR WAS DAERON'S FOURTH SON, AND AEMON WAS MAEKAR'S THIRD SON.

MAESTER AEMON WAS NAMED FOR THE DRAGONKNIGHT.

YES. BUT OUR AEMON LACKED THE DRAGONKNIGHT'S MARTIAL NATURE.

HE LIKES TO SAY HE HAD A SLOW SWORD BUT QUICK WITS. SMALL WONDER HIS GRANDFATHER PACKED HIM OFF TO THE CITADEL.

YET ONE BY ONE ALL HIS ROYAL UNCLES AND THEIR HEIRS PERISHED, UNTIL HIS FATHER MAEKAR SAT THE IRON THRONE.

AND THEN, WITH MAEKAR AND HIS ELDER SONS DEAD, THE CROWN WAS OFFERED, QUIETLY, TO AEMON. AND QUIETLY HE REFUSED. THE GODS MEANT FOR HIM TO SERVE, NOT TO RULE, HE SAID.

SO THE CROWN WENT TO AEMON'S YOUNGER BROTHER—AEGON, THE FIFTH OF HIS NAME. AEGON THE UNLIKELY, THEY CALLED HIM, BORN THE FOURTH SON OF A FOURTH SON.

AEMON KNEW THAT IF HE REMAINED AT COURT, THOSE WHO DISLIKED HIS BROTHER'S RULE WOULD SEEK TO USE HIM, SO HE CAME TO THE WALL.

AND HERE HE HAS REMAINED, WHILE HIS BROTHER AND HIS BROTHER'S SON AND *HIS* SON EACH REIGNED AND DIED IN TURN, UNTIL JAIME LANNISTER PUT AN END TO THE LINE OF THE DRAGONKINGS.

KING. KING.

THE REALM HAS THREE KINGS ALREADY, AND THAT'S TWO TOO MANY FOR MY LIKING.

MY LORD, WHY HAVE YOU TOLD ME THIS?

YOUR BROTHER ROBB HAS BEEN CROWNED KING IN THE NORTH. YOU AND AEMON HAVE THAT IN COMMON. A KING FOR A BROTHER.

AND THIS TOO. A VOW.

GIVE ME A MAN FOR EVERY VOW I'VE SEEN BROKEN AND THE WALL WILL NEVER LACK FOR DEFENDERS.

I'VE ALWAYS KNOWN THAT ROBB WOULD BE LORD OF WINTERFELL.

A LORD'S ONE THING, A KING'S ANOTHER.

THEY WILL GARB YOUR BROTHER IN SILKS, WHILE YOU LIVE AND DIE IN BLACK RINGMAIL. ROBB WILL RULE, YOU WILL SERVE.

TELL ME THAT NONE OF THIS TROUBLES YOU, JON...AND I'LL NAME YOU A LIAR.

AND IF IT DID TROUBLE ME, WHAT MIGHT I DO, BASTARD AS I AM?

WHAT WILL YOU DO? BASTARD AS YOU ARE?

BE TROUBLED. AND KEEP MY VOWS.

HER GRACE LEFT ORDERS.

THE COUNCIL IN SESSION IS NOT TO BE DISTURBED.

JAIME HAD ONCE TOLD TYRION THAT THAT SER MANDON MOORE WAS THE MOST DANGEROUS OF THE KINGSGUARD, BECAUSE HIS FACE GAVE NO HINT OF WHAT HE MIGHT DO NEXT.

I WOULD BE ONLY A SMALL DISTURBANCE.

I BEAR A LETTER FROM MY FATHER, LORD TYWIN LANNISTER, THE HAND OF THE KING.

HER GRACE DOES NOT WISH TO BE DISTURBED.

SER MANDON, YOU HAVE NOT MET MY COMPANIONS. THIS IS BRONN. PERCHANCE YOU RECALL SER VARDIS EGEN, WHO WAS CAPTAIN OF LORD ARRYN'S HOUSEHOLD GUARD?

I KNOW THE MAN.

KNEW.

BE THAT AS IT MAY, I MUST SEE MY SISTER. IF YOU WOULD BE SO KIND AS TO OPEN THE DOOR?

YOU MAY ENTER. THEY MAY NOT.

A SMALL VICTORY, BUT SWEET. HE HAD PASSED HIS FIRST TEST.

YOU.

I CAN SEE WHERE JOFFREY LEARNED HIS COURTESIES.

WHAT ARE YOU DOING HERE?

DELIVERING A LETTER FROM OUR LORD FATHER.

HOW KIND OF LORD TYWIN. AND HIS SEALING WAX IS SUCH A LOVELY SHADE OF GOLD. IT GIVES EVERY APPEARANCE OF BEING GENUINE.

OF COURSE IT'S GENUINE.

THIS IS ABSURD! MY LORD FATHER HAS SENT MY BROTHER TO SIT IN HIS PLACE. HE BIDS US ACCEPT TYRION AS THE HAND OF THE KING, UNTIL SUCH TIME AS HE HIMSELF CAN JOIN US.

IT WOULD SEEM THAT A WELCOME IS IN ORDER.

INDEED. WE HAVE SORE NEED OF YOU, MY LORD. REBELLION EVERYWHERE, THIS GRIM OMEN IN THE SKY, RIOTING IN THE CITY STREETS...

AND WHOSE FAULT IS THAT, LORD JANOS? YOUR GOLD CLOAKS ARE CHARGED WITH KEEPING ORDER. AS TO YOU, TYRION, YOU COULD BETTER SERVE US ON THE FIELD OF BATTLE.

NO, I'M DONE WITH FIELDS OF BATTLE, THANK YOU. I SIT A CHAIR BETTER THAN A HORSE, AND I'D SOONER HOLD A WINE GOBLET THAN A BATTLE-AXE.

WELL SAID, LANNISTER. A MAN AFTER MY OWN HEART.

PLEASE, DO LET ME BE OF SERVICE, IN WHATEVER *SMALL* WAY I CAN.

HOW MANY MEN HAVE YOU BROUGHT WITH YOU?

A FEW HUNDRED. MY OWN MEN, CHIEFLY. FATHER WAS LOATH TO PART WITH ANY OF HIS. HE IS FIGHTING A WAR.

WHAT USE WILL YOUR FEW HUNDRED MEN BE IF RENLY MARCHES ON THE CITY, OR STANNIS SAILS FROM DRAGONSTONE?

I ASK FOR AN ARMY AND MY FATHER SENDS ME A DWARF. THE *KING* NAMES THE HAND, AND JOFFREY NAMED OUR LORD FATHER.

AND OUR LORD FATHER NAMED ME.

HE CANNOT DO THAT. NOT WITHOUT JOFF'S CONSENT!

LORD TYWIN IS AT HARRENHAL WITH HIS HOST, IF YOU'D CARE TO TAKE IT UP WITH HIM.

MY LORDS, PERCHANCE YOU WOULD PERMIT ME A PRIVATE WORD WITH MY SISTER?

HOW YOU MUST HAVE YEARNED FOR THE SOUND OF YOUR SWEET SISTER'S VOICE. MY LORDS, PLEASE, LET US GIVE THEM A FEW MOMENTS TOGETHER. THE WOES OF OUR TROUBLED REALM SHALL KEEP.

SHALL I TELL THE STEWARD TO PREPARE CHAMBERS IN MAEGOR'S HOLDFAST?

MY THANKS, LORD PETYR, BUT I WILL BE TAKING LORD STARK'S FORMER QUARTERS IN THE TOWER OF THE HAND.

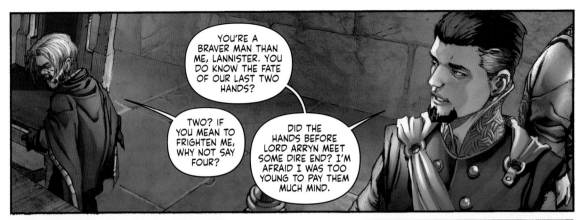

YOU'RE A BRAVER MAN THAN ME, LANNISTER. YOU DO KNOW THE FATE OF OUR LAST TWO HANDS?

TWO? IF YOU MEAN TO FRIGHTEN ME, WHY NOT SAY FOUR?

DID THE HANDS BEFORE LORD ARRYN MEET SOME DIRE END? I'M AFRAID I WAS TOO YOUNG TO PAY THEM MUCH MIND.

AERYS TARGARYEN'S LAST HAND WAS KILLED DURING THE SACK OF KING'S LANDING. THE ONE BEFORE HIM WAS BURNED TO DEATH. AND BEFORE THEM CAME TWO OTHERS WHO DIED LANDLESS AND PENNILESS IN EXILE.

I BELIEVE MY LORD FATHER WAS THE LAST HAND TO DEPART KING'S LANDING WITH HIS NAME, PROPERTIES, AND PARTS ALL INTACT.

BUT WHATEVER CURSE MAY LINGER OVER THE TOWER OF THE HAND, I PRAY I'M SMALL ENOUGH TO ESCAPE ITS NOTICE.

I HOPE FATHER DID NOT SEND YOU ALL THIS WAY TO PLAGUE US WITH HISTORY LESSONS.

HOW I HAVE YEARNED FOR THE SOUND OF YOUR SWEET VOICE.

HOW I HAVE YEARNED TO HAVE THAT EUNUCH'S TONGUE PULLED OUT WITH HOT PINCERS! HAS FATHER LOST HIS SENSES? OR DID YOU FORGE THIS LETTER?

WHY WOULD HE INFLICT YOU ON ME? I DO NOT REQUIRE YOUR HELP. IT WAS OUR FATHER'S PRESENCE THAT I COMMANDED.

YES, BUT IT'S JAIME YOU WANT.

JAIME—

—IS MY BROTHER NO LESS THAN YOURS. GIVE ME YOUR SUPPORT, AND WE WILL HAVE JAIME FREED AND RETURNED TO US UNHARMED.

HOW? THE STARK BOY AND HIS MOTHER ARE NOT LIKE TO FORGET WE BEHEADED LORD EDDARD.

TRUE, YET YOU STILL HOLD HIS DAUGHTERS, DON'T YOU?

SANSA. I'VE GIVEN IT OUT THAT I HAVE THE YOUNGER BRAT AS WELL, BUT IT'S A LIE.

TELL ME ABOUT OUR FRIENDS ON THE COUNCIL. ARE YOU CERTAIN OF THEIR LOYALTY? DO YOU TRUST THEM?

I TRUST NO ONE. I NEED THEM. DOES FATHER BELIEVE THEY ARE PLAYING US FALSE?

HE KNOWS THAT YOUR SON'S SHORT REIGN HAS BEEN A LONG PARADE OF FOLLIES AND DISASTERS. THAT SUGGESTS THAT SOMEONE IS GIVING JOFFREY SOME VERY BAD COUNSEL.

JOFF HAS HAD NO LACK OF GOOD COUNSEL. BUT NOW THAT HE'S KING, HE BELIEVES HE SHOULD DO AS HE PLEASES, NOT AS HE'S BID.

CROWNS DO QUEER THINGS TO THE HEADS BENEATH THEM. THIS BUSINESS WITH EDDARD STARK...JOFFREY'S WORK?

HE WAS INSTRUCTED TO PARDON STARK, ALLOW HIM TO TAKE THE BLACK. THE MAN WOULD HAVE BEEN OUT OF OUR WAY, AND WE MIGHT HAVE MADE PEACE WITH THAT SON OF HIS, BUT JOFF...

HE CALLED FOR LORD EDDARD'S HEAD IN FRONT OF HALF THE CITY. AND JANOS SLYNT AND SER ILYN WENT AHEAD AND BLITHELY SHORTENED THE MAN WITHOUT A WORD FROM ME!

SO THIS LORD SLYNT, HE WAS PART OF IT? TELL ME, WHOSE FINE NOTION WAS IT TO GRANT HIM HARRENHAL AND NAME HIM TO THE COUNCIL?

LITTLEFINGER MADE THE ARRANGEMENTS. WE NEEDED SLYNT'S GOLD CLOAKS. EDDARD STARK HAD WRITTEN TO LORD STANNIS, OFFERING HIM THE THRONE.

IF SANSA HADN'T TOLD ME ALL HER FATHER'S PLANS...

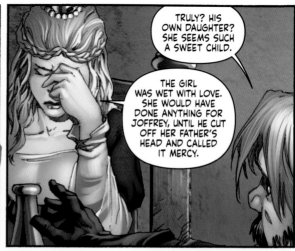

TRULY? HIS OWN DAUGHTER? SHE SEEMS SUCH A SWEET CHILD.

THE GIRL WAS WET WITH LOVE. SHE WOULD HAVE DONE ANYTHING FOR JOFFREY, UNTIL HE CUT OFF HER FATHER'S HEAD AND CALLED IT MERCY.

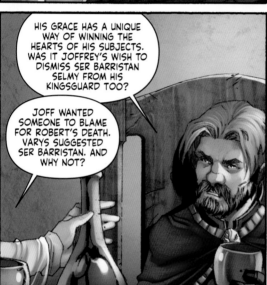

HIS GRACE HAS A UNIQUE WAY OF WINNING THE HEARTS OF HIS SUBJECTS. WAS IT JOFFREY'S WISH TO DISMISS SER BARRISTAN SELMY FROM HIS KINGSGUARD TOO?

JOFF WANTED SOMEONE TO BLAME FOR ROBERT'S DEATH. VARYS SUGGESTED SER BARRISTAN. AND WHY NOT?

BECAUSE THE SMALLFOLK REVERE HIM.

WHAT DO YOU IMAGINE THEY'LL THINK WHEN THEY SEE BARRISTAN THE BOLD RIDING BESIDE ROBB STARK OR STANNIS BARATHEON?

I HAD NOT CONSIDERED THAT.

FATHER DID. THAT IS WHY HE SENT ME. TO PUT AN END TO THESE FOLLIES AND BRING YOUR SON TO HEEL.

JOFF WILL BE NO MORE TRACTABLE FOR YOU THAN FOR ME.

HE MIGHT. HE KNOWS YOU WOULD NEVER HURT HIM.

IF YOU BELIEVE I'D EVER ALLOW YOU TO HARM MY SON, YOU'RE SICK WITH FEVER!

JOFFREY IS AS SAFE WITH ME AS HE IS WITH YOU, BUT SO LONG AS THE BOY *FEELS* THREATENED, HE'LL BE MORE INCLINED TO LISTEN.

I AM YOUR BROTHER, YOU KNOW. YOU NEED ME, WHETHER YOU ADMIT IT OR NO. AND YOUR SON NEEDS ME, IF HE'S TO HAVE A HOPE OF RETAINING THAT UGLY IRON CHAIR.

YOU HAVE ALWAYS BEEN CUNNING.

IN MY OWN SMALL WAY.

IT MAY BE WORTH THE TRYING... BUT IF I ACCEPT YOU, YOU WILL DO *NOTHING* WITHOUT MY CONSENT. DO YOU UNDERSTAND?

CERTAINLY. AND AS WE OUGHT HAVE NO MORE SECRETS BETWEEN US...

...WHO MURDERED JON ARRYN?

THE GRIEVING WIDOW IN THE EYRIE SEEMS TO THINK IT WAS ME.

WHERE DID SHE COME BY THAT NOTION, I WONDER?

I'M SURE I DON'T KNOW. THAT FOOL EDDARD STARK ACCUSED ME OF THE SAME THING. HE HINTED THAT LORD ARRYN SUSPECTED...

THAT YOU WERE FUCKING OUR SWEET JAIME?

PAK

DID YOU THINK I WAS AS BLIND AS FATHER? WHO YOU LIE WITH IS NO MATTER TO ME... ALTHOUGH IT DOESN'T SEEM QUITE JUST THAT YOU SHOULD OPEN YOUR LEGS FOR ONE BROTHER AND NOT THE OTHER.

PAK

BE GENTLE, CERSEI, I'M ONLY JESTING. AND IF YOU KEEP DOING THAT, I MIGHT GET ANGRY.

HOW DID YOU KILL ROBERT?

HE DID THAT HIMSELF. ALL WE DID WAS HELP. WHEN LANCEL SAW THAT ROBERT WAS GOING AFTER BOAR, HE GAVE HIM STRONGWINE—THREE TIMES AS POTENT AS HE WAS USED TO.

HE COULD HAVE STOPPED SWILLING IT DOWN ANYTIME HE CARED TO, BUT NO, HE DRAINED ONE SKIN AND TOLD LANCEL TO FETCH ANOTHER. THE BOAR DID THE REST.

YOU SHOULD HAVE BEEN AT THE FEAST. THERE HAS NEVER BEEN A BOAR SO DELICIOUS. THEY COOKED IT WITH MUSHROOMS AND APPLES, AND IT TASTED LIKE TRIUMPH!

TRULY, SISTER, YOU WERE BORN TO BE A WIDOW.

NOW, IF YOU ARE DONE SLAPPING ME, I WILL BE OFF.

I HAVEN'T GIVEN YOU LEAVE TO DEPART! I WANT TO KNOW HOW YOU INTEND TO FREE JAIME.

I'LL TELL YOU WHEN I KNOW. SCHEMES ARE LIKE FRUIT, THEY REQUIRE A CERTAIN RIPENING.

RIGHT NOW, I HAVE A MIND TO RIDE THROUGH THE STREETS AND TAKE THE MEASURE OF THIS CITY.

I WANT THOSE TAKEN DOWN ON THE MORROW.

IT WOULD BE HELL TO MATCH THEM WITH THE BODIES, BUT CERTAIN DECENCIES MUST BE OBSERVED.

HIS GRACE HAS TOLD US HE WISHES THE HEADS TO REMAIN UNTIL HE FILLS THOSE LAST THREE SPIKES.

PRESUMABLY ONE IS FOR ROBB STARK, AND THE OTHERS FOR LORDS STANNIS AND RENLY? TRY AND RECALL THAT MY NEPHEW IS STILL A CHILD.

THERE IS NO FOOD COMING IN, IS THERE?

LITTLE ENOUGH. WITH THE WAR IN THE RIVERLANDS AND LORD RENLY RAISING REBELS IN HIGHGARDEN, THE ROADS ARE CLOSED TO THE SOUTH AND WEST.

LORD LITTLEFINGER HAS IMPOSED A TAX ON THOSE WISHING TO ENTER THE CITY.

FRESH RATS! FRESH RATS!

LATER.

MY GOOD LORD, I AM SO PLEASED TO SEE YOU.

LORD VARYS. I HAD NOT THOUGHT TO SEE YOU HERE.

FORGIVE ME IF I INTRUDE. I WAS TAKEN BY A SUDDEN URGE TO MEET YOUR YOUNG LADY.

YOUNG LADY. YOU'RE HALF RIGHT, M'LORD. I'M YOUNG.

OTHERS TAKE HIM, HOW DID HE FIND THEM SO QUICKLY?

I FEAR I'M THE INTRUDER, LORD VARYS. WHEN I CAME IN, YOU WERE IN THE MIDST OF SOME MERRIMENT.

WILL YOU TAKE SOME WINE WITH US, MY LORD?

I ALWAYS LIKE TO RETURN TO THE CITY THROUGH THE GATE OF THE GODS. THE CARVINGS ON THE GATEHOUSE ARE EXQUISITE. THE EYES...SO EXPRESSIVE. THEY ALMOST SEEM TO FOLLOW YOU AS YOU RIDE BENEATH.

I NEVER NOTICED, M'LORD. I'LL LOOK AGAIN ON THE MORROW, IF IT PLEASE YOU.

YOUR YOUNG LADY HAS AN AMIABLE WAY TO HER. I SHOULD TAKE VERY GOOD CARE OF HER IF I WERE YOU.

I INTEND TO.

I WILL LEAVE YOU. I KNOW HOW WEARY YOU MUST BE. I ONLY WISHED TO WELCOME YOU, AND TELL YOU HOW VERY PLEASED I AM BY YOUR ARRIVAL.

MAY I LEAVE YOU WITH A BIT OF A RIDDLE, LORD TYRION?

IN A ROOM SIT THREE GREAT MEN: A KING, A PRIEST, AND A RICH MAN WITH HIS GOLD. BETWEEN THEM STANDS A SELLSWORD, A LITTLE MAN OF COMMON BIRTH AND NO GREAT MIND. EACH OF THE GREAT ONES BIDS HIM SLAY THE OTHER TWO.

"DO IT," SAYS THE KING, *"FOR I AM YOUR LAWFUL RULER."* *"DO IT,"* SAYS THE PRIEST, *"FOR I COMMAND YOU IN THE NAMES OF THE GODS."* *"DO IT,"* SAYS THE RICH MAN, *"AND ALL THIS GOLD SHALL BE YOURS."* SO TELL ME—WHO LIVES AND WHO DIES?

THE RICH MAN LIVES. DOESN'T HE?

THAT WOULD DEPEND ON THE SELLSWORD, IT SEEMS. COME, LET'S GO UPSTAIRS.

MY LION. MY SWEET LORD, MY GIANT OF LANNISTER.

SO WHAT WILL YOU DO, M'LORD, NOW THAT YOU'RE THE HAND OF THE KING?

SOMETHING CERSEI WILL NEVER EXPECT.

I'LL DO... JUSTICE.

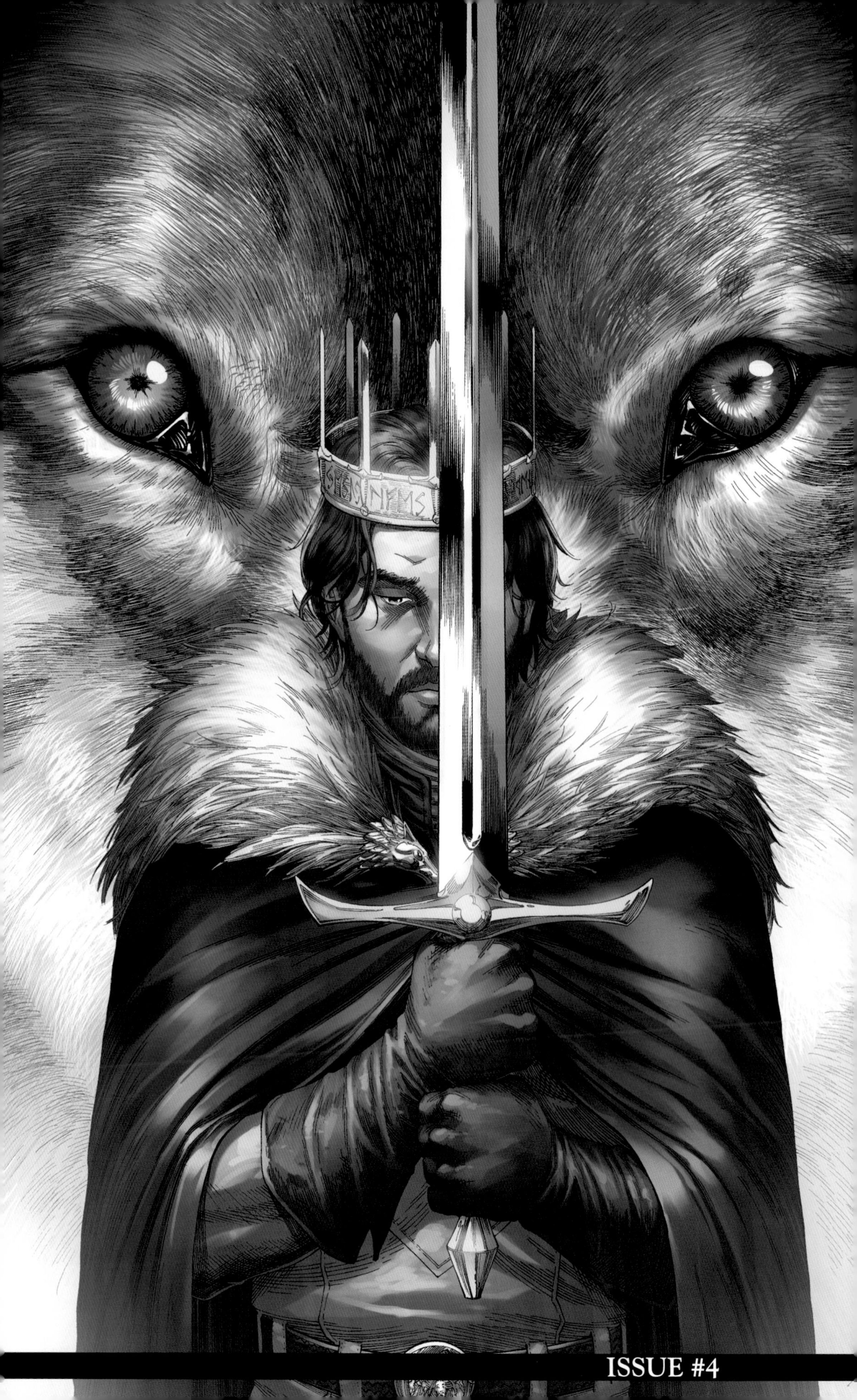

ISSUE #4

ARYA

YOREN AND HIS CHARGES TRAVELED DAWN TO DUSK, PAST WOODS AND ORCHARDS AND NEATLY TENDED FIELDS, THROUGH SMALL VILLAGES, CROWDED MARKET TOWNS, AND STOUT HOLDFASTS.

COME DARK, THEY WOULD MAKE CAMP AND EAT BY THE LIGHT OF THE RED SWORD.

THERE SEEMED TO BE MORE TRAFFIC ON THE KINGSROAD EVERY DAY.

MORN, NOON AND NIGHT THEY CAME. SOME DROVE FARM WAGONS OR BUMPED ALONG IN THE BACK OF OX CARTS. MORE RODE.

BUT MOST CAME ON FOOT, WITH THEIR GOODS ON THEIR SHOULDERS AND WEARY, WARY LOOKS UPON THEIR FACES. THEY WALKED SOUTH, TOWARD THE CITY, TOWARD KING'S LANDING.

ONLY ONE IN A HUNDRED SPARED SO MUCH AS A WORD FOR YOREN AND HIS CHARGES, AND ARYA WONDERED WHY NO ONE ELSE WAS GOING THE SAME WAY AS THEM.

ARYA NOTICED THE FIRST GRAVE NOT LONG AFTER: A SMALL MOUND BESIDE THE ROAD, DUG FOR A CHILD. A CRYSTAL HAD BEEN SET IN THE SOFT EARTH, AND LOMMY WANTED TO TAKE IT UNTIL THE BULL TOLD HIM HE'D BETTER LEAVE THE DEAD ALONE.

A FEW LEAGUES FARTHER ON, THERE WERE MORE GRAVES, A WHOLE ROW, FRESHLY DUG. AFTER THAT, A DAY HARDLY PASSED WITHOUT ONE.

THERE'S NO GOING NORTH. HALF THE FIELDS ARE BURNT, AND WHAT FOLKS ARE LEFT ARE WALLED UP INSIDE THEIR HOLDFASTS. ONE BUNCH RIDES OFF AT DAWN AND ANOTHER ONE SHOWS UP BY DUSK.

THAT'S NOTHING TO US. TULLY OR LANNISTER, MAKES NO MATTER. THE WATCH TAKES NO PART.

THERE'S WILD MEN DOWN FROM THE MOUNTAINS OF THE MOON, TRY TELLING *THEM* YOU TAKE NO PART. AND THE STARKS ARE IN IT TOO, THE YOUNG LORD'S COME DOWN, THE DEAD HAND'S SON...

DID HE MEAN *ROBB*?

I HEARD THE BOY RIDES TO BATTLE ON A WOLF! THE MAN I HEARD IT FROM, HE SAW IT HIMSELF. A WOLF BIG AS A HORSE, HE SWORE.

THAT'S FOOLS TALK.

IT'S BEEN A BAD YEAR FOR WOLVES. AROUND THE GODS EYE, THE PACKS HAVE GROWN BOLDER'N ANYONE CAN REMEMBER. THEY GOT NO FEAR OF MEN.

I HEARD THE SAME THING FROM MY COUSIN. SHE SAYS THERE'S THIS GREAT PACK, HUNDREDS OF THEM, MANKILLERS. THE ONE THAT LEADS THEM IS A SHE-WOLF, A BITCH FROM THE SEVENTH HELL.

WAS THE GODS EYE NEAR THE TRIDENT? IT WAS NEAR THE TRIDENT THAT ARYA HAD LEFT NYMERIA.

SHE HADN'T WANTED TO, BUT JORY SAID THEY HAD NO CHOICE, THAT THE WOLF WOULD BE KILLED FOR BITING JOFFREY, EVEN IF HE DESERVED IT.

THEY'D HAD TO SHOUT AND SCREAM AND THROW STONES UNTIL THE DIREWOLF FINALLY STOPPED FOLLOWING THEM.

I HEARD HOW THIS HELLBITCH WALKED INTO A VILLAGE ONE DAY...A MARKET DAY, PEOPLE EVERYWHERE, AND TEARS A BABY FROM HIS MOTHER'S ARMS, BOLD AS YOU PLEASE.

THAT'S JUST A STORY! WOLVES DON'T EAT BABIES!

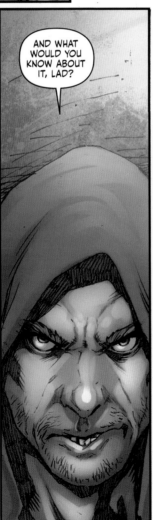

AND WHAT WOULD YOU KNOW ABOUT IT, LAD?

THE BOY'S GREENSICK ON BEER, THAT'S ALL.

NO I'M NOT. THEY *DON'T* EAT BABIES...

OUTSIDE, *BOY*... SEE THAT THE STABLEBOY HAS WATERED OUR HORSES. AND STAY THERE UNTIL YOU LEARN TO SHUT YOUR MOUTH WHEN MEN ARE TALKING.

THEY *DON'T*.

BOY.

LOVELY BOY.

A MAN COULD USE ANOTHER TASTE OF BEER. A MAN HAS A THIRST, WEARING THESE HEAVY BRACELETS.

A BOY COULD MAKE A FRIEND.

I HAVE FRIENDS.

NONE I CAN SEE.

HSSS!

STOP THAT!

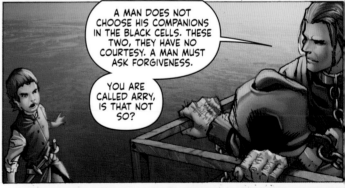

A MAN DOES NOT CHOOSE HIS COMPANIONS IN THE BLACK CELLS. THESE TWO, THEY HAVE NO COURTESY. A MAN MUST ASK FORGIVENESS.

YOU ARE CALLED ARRY, IS THAT NOT SO?

LUMPYHEAD. LUMPYHEAD LUMPYFACE STICKBOY.

HAVE A CARE, LORATH, HE'LL HIT YOU WITH HIS STICK.

THIS MAN HAS THE HONOR TO BE JAQEN H'GHAR, ONCE OF THE FREE CITY OF LORATH. WOULD THAT HE WERE HOME.

THIS MAN'S ILL-BRED COMPANIONS IN CAPTIVITY ARE NAMED RORGE AND BITER.

HSSS...

BITER CANNOT SPEAK AND BITER CANNOT WRITE, YET HIS TEETH ARE VERY SHARP, SO A MAN CALLS HIM BITER. ARE YOU CHARMED?

NO.

YOU GET US SOME BEER, PIMPLE. NOW!

ARYA TRIED TO THINK WHAT SYRIO WOULD HAVE DONE. SHE DREW HER WOODEN PRACTICE SWORD.

ARYA MADE HERSELF APPROACH THE WAGON. EACH STEP WAS HARDER THAN THE ONE BEFORE.

FEAR CUTS DEEPER THAN SWORDS.

FIERCE AS A WOLVERINE, CALM AS STILL WATER.

THWACK

WHAT ARE YOU DOING?

A BOY HAS MORE COURAGE THAN SENSE.

YOREN SAID NONE OF US SHOULD GO NEAR THOSE THREE.

THEY DON'T SCARE ME.

THEN YOU'RE STUPID. THEY SCARE ME.

LET'S GET AWAY FROM HERE.

RORGE'S LAUGHTER AND BITER'S HISSING FOLLOWED THEM. ARYA WANTED TO HIT SOMETHING.

WANT TO FIGHT?

WHAT'S WRONG?

"GOLD CLOAKS."

WHAT IS IT? WHAT ARE YOU DOING? LET GO.

QUIET AS A SHADOW.

I HAVE A WARRANT FOR A CERTAIN BOY—

WHO IS IT WANTS THIS BOY?

THE QUEEN WANTS HIM, OLD MAN, NOT THAT IT'S YOUR CONCERN.

WHY ARE WE HIDING?

IT'S ME THEY WANT. YOU BE QUIET.

YOU'LL HAVE NO ONE. THE BOY'S IN THE NIGHT'S WATCH NOW. THERE'S LAWS ON SUCH THINGS.

HERE'S YOUR LAW.

THAT'S NO LAW, JUST A SWORD. HAPPENS I GOT ONE TOO.

OLD FOOL. I HAVE FIVE MEN WITH ME.

HAPPENS I GOT THIRTY.

THIS LOT? WHO'S FIRST?

I AM.

NO, I AM.

ME.

ME AND HIM.

ALL OF US.

IS IT A FIGHT?

I GUESS.

ARYA COULD NOT BELIEVE IT. SHE **HATED** HOT PIE! WHY WOULD HE RISK HIMSELF FOR HER?

YOU GIRLS PUT AWAY THEM ROCKS AND STICKS BEFORE YOU GET SPANKED. NONE OF YOU KNOWS WHAT END OF A SWORD TO HOLD.

I DO!

HA!

PUT THE BLADE AWAY, LITTLE GIRL, NO ONE WANTS TO HURT YOU.

I'M *NOT* A GIRL! I'M THE ONE YOU WANT.

HE'S THE ONE WE WANT.

NEITHER'S THE ONE YOU GET. I GOT ME TEN, FIFTEEN MORE BROTHERS IN THAT INN, IF YOU STILL NEED CONVINCING.

I WAS YOU, I'D LET LOOSE OF THAT GUTCUTTER, SPREAD MY CHEEKS OVER THAT FAT LITTLE HORSE, AND GALLOP ON BACK TO THE CITY.

NOW.

WE'LL JUST KEEP THAT. GOOD STEEL'S ALWAYS NEEDED ON THE WALL.

AS YOU SAY. FOR NOW. MEN.

YOU'D BEST SCAMPER UP TO THAT WALL OF YOURS IN A HURRY, OLD MAN. THE NEXT TIME I CATCH YOU, I BELIEVE I'LL HAVE YOUR HEAD TO GO WITH THE BASTARD BOY'S.

BETTER MEN THAN YOU HAVE TRIED.

WOOOOO!

FOOL! YOU THINK HE'S DONE WITH US? NEXT TIME HE WON'T PRANCE UP AND HAND ME NO DAMN RIBBON.

WE NEED TO BE MOVING. RIDE ALL NIGHT, MAYBE WE CAN STAY AHEAD O' THEM FOR A BIT.

QUEEN WANTS YOU BAD, BOY.

WHY SHOULD SHE WANT *HIM?*

WHY SHOULD SHE WANT *YOU?* YOU'RE NOTHING BUT A LITTLE GUTTER RAT!

WELL, YOU'RE NOTHING BUT A BASTARD BOY!

WHAT'S YOUR TRUE NAME?

GENDRY.

DON'T SEE WHY NO ONE WANTS NEITHER O' YOU, BUT THEY CAN'T HAVE YOU REGARDLESS.

YOU RIDE THEM TWO COURSERS. FIRST SIGHT OF A GOLD CLOAK, MAKE FOR THE WALL LIKE A DRAGON'S ON YOUR TAIL. THE REST O' US DON'T MEAN SPIT TO THEM.

EXCEPT FOR YOU. THAT MAN SAID HE'D TAKE YOUR HEAD TOO.

WELL, AS TO THAT, IF HE CAN GET IT OFF MY SHOULDERS, HE'S WELCOME TO IT.

CATELYN

RISE, SER CLEOS.

I BROUGHT YOU FROM YOUR CELL TO CARRY MY MESSAGE TO YOUR COUSIN CERSEI LANNISTER IN KING'S LANDING.

YOU'LL TRAVEL UNDER A PEACE BANNER, WITH THIRTY OF MY BEST MEN TO ESCORT YOU.

HER SON'S CROWN WAS FRESH FROM THE FORGE, AND IT SEEMED TO CATELYN STARK THAT THE WEIGHT OF IT PRESSED HEAVY ON ROBB'S HEAD.

I SHOULD BE MOST GLAD TO BRING HIS GRACE'S MESSAGE TO THE QUEEN.

UNDERSTAND...I AM NOT GIVING YOU YOUR FREEDOM. I WANT YOUR PLEDGE, ON YOUR HONOR AS A KNIGHT, THAT YOU'LL RETURN WITH THE QUEEN'S REPLY, AND RESUME YOUR CAPTIVITY.

I...DO SO VOW. WHAT IS THIS MESSAGE?

AN OFFER OF PEACE. IF THE QUEEN REGENT MEETS MY TERMS, I WILL SHEATH THIS SWORD AND MAKE AN END TO THE WAR BETWEEN US.

FIRST, THE QUEEN MUST RELEASE MY SISTERS AND PROVIDE THEM WITH TRANSPORT TO WHITE HARBOR. SANSA'S BETROTHAL TO JOFFREY BARATHEON IS AT AN END.

WHEN I RECEIVE WORD FROM MY CASTELLAN THAT MY SISTERS HAVE RETURNED UNHARMED TO WINTERFELL, I WILL RELEASE THE QUEEN'S COUSINS AND GIVE THEM SAFE ESCORT TO WHERESOEVER SHE DESIRES THEM DELIVERED.

SECONDLY, MY LORD FATHER'S BONES WILL BE RETURNED TO US, ALONG WITH THE REMAINS OF HIS HOUSEHOLD GUARD WHO DIED IN HIS SERVICE AT KING'S LANDING.

LIVING MEN HAD GONE SOUTH, AND COLD BONES WOULD RETURN.

NED HAD THE TRUTH OF IT. HIS PLACE WAS AT WINTERFELL, BUT WOULD I HEAR HIM? GO, I TOLD HIM, YOU MUST BE ROBERT'S HAND, FOR THE GOOD OF OUR HOUSE, FOR THE SAKE OF OUR CHILDREN... MY DOING, MINE, NO OTHER...

THIRD, MY FATHER'S GREATSWORD ICE WILL BE DELIVERED TO MY HAND, HERE AT RIVERRUN.

FOURTH, THE QUEEN WILL COMMAND HER FATHER LORD TYWIN TO RELEASE THOSE KNIGHTS AND LORDS BANNERMEN OF MINE THAT HE TOOK CAPTIVE.

ONCE HE DOES SO, I SHALL RELEASE MY OWN CAPTIVES, SAVE JAIME LANNISTER ALONE, WHO WILL REMAIN MY HOSTAGE FOR HIS FATHER'S GOOD BEHAVIOR.

LASTLY, KING JOFFREY AND THE QUEEN REGENT MUST RENOUNCE ALL CLAIMS TO DOMINION OVER THE NORTH. HENCEFORTH WE ARE NO PART OF THEIR REALM, BUT A FREE AND INDEPENDENT KINGDOM, AS OF OLD.

MAESTER VYMAN HAS DRAWN A MAP, SHOWING THE BORDERS WE CLAIM.

THOSE ARE THE TERMS. IF SHE MEETS THEM, I'LL GIVE HER PEACE. IF NOT...

...I'LL GIVE HER ANOTHER WHISPERING WOOD.

STARK! KING IN THE NORTH!

THE KING IN THE NORTH!

YOU DID WELL. THOUGH THAT BUSINESS WITH THE WOLF WAS MORE BEFITTING A BOY THAN A KING.

DID YOU SEE THE LOOK ON CLEOS'S FACE, MOTHER?

WHAT I SAW WAS LORD KARSTARK, WALKING OUT.

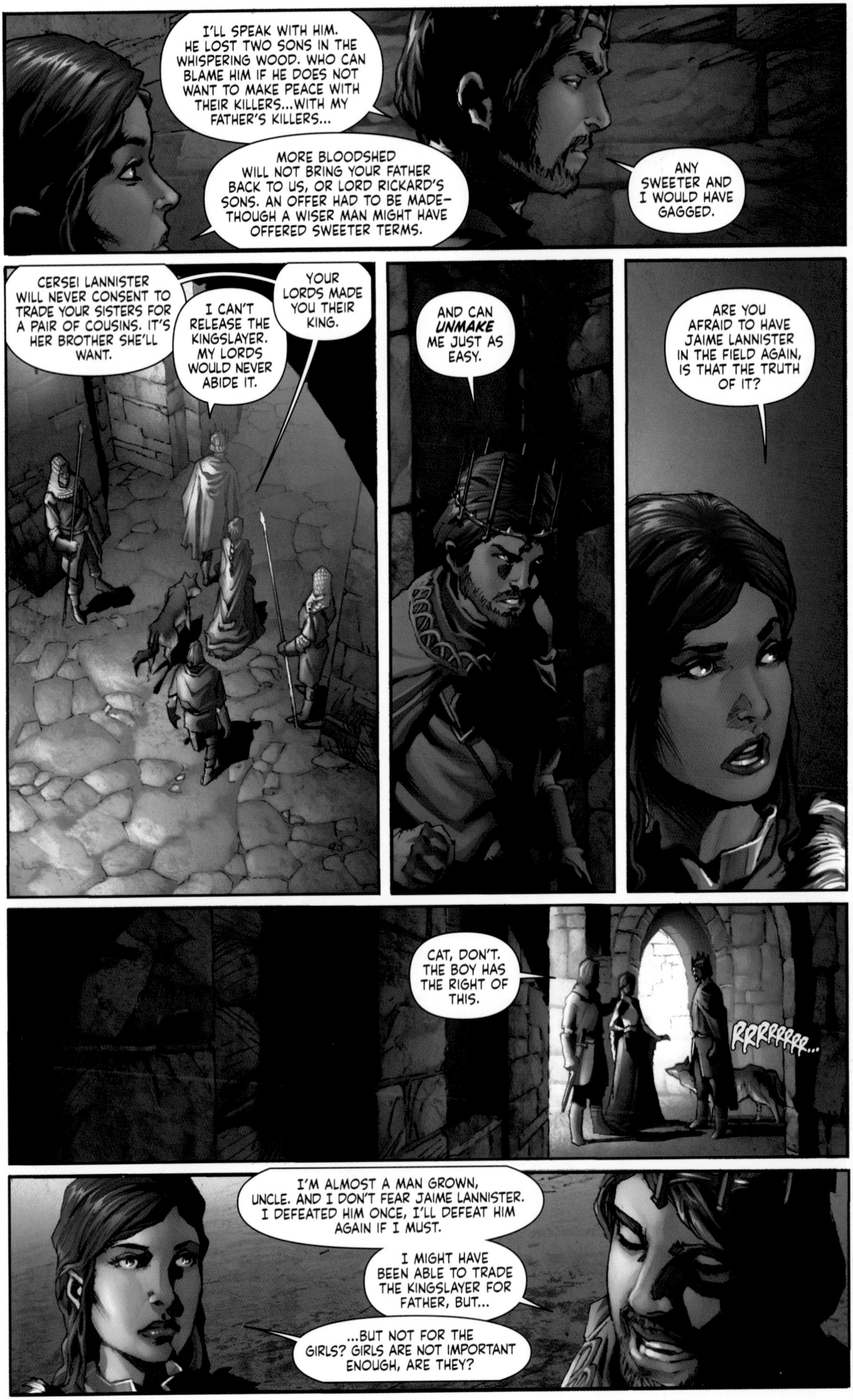
I'LL SPEAK WITH HIM. HE LOST TWO SONS IN THE WHISPERING WOOD. WHO CAN BLAME HIM IF HE DOES NOT WANT TO MAKE PEACE WITH THEIR KILLERS...WITH MY FATHER'S KILLERS...
MORE BLOODSHED WILL NOT BRING YOUR FATHER BACK TO US, OR LORD RICKARD'S SONS. AN OFFER HAD TO BE MADE—THOUGH A WISER MAN MIGHT HAVE OFFERED SWEETER TERMS.
ANY SWEETER AND I WOULD HAVE GAGGED.
CERSEI LANNISTER WILL NEVER CONSENT TO TRADE YOUR SISTERS FOR A PAIR OF COUSINS. IT'S HER BROTHER SHE'LL WANT.
I CAN'T RELEASE THE KINGSLAYER. MY LORDS WOULD NEVER ABIDE IT.
YOUR LORDS MADE YOU THEIR KING.
AND CAN *UNMAKE* ME JUST AS EASY.
ARE YOU AFRAID TO HAVE JAIME LANNISTER IN THE FIELD AGAIN, IS THAT THE TRUTH OF IT?
CAT, DON'T. THE BOY HAS THE RIGHT OF THIS.
RRRRRRRR...
I'M ALMOST A MAN GROWN, UNCLE. AND I DON'T FEAR JAIME LANNISTER. I DEFEATED HIM ONCE, I'LL DEFEAT HIM AGAIN IF I MUST.
I MIGHT HAVE BEEN ABLE TO TRADE THE KINGSLAYER FOR FATHER, BUT...
...BUT NOT FOR THE GIRLS? GIRLS ARE NOT IMPORTANT ENOUGH, ARE THEY?

I'LL DO ALL I CAN FOR MY SISTERS.

ARE YOU SURE YOU WON'T CONSENT TO GO WITH THEON? HE LEAVES ON THE MORROW FOR THE IRON ISLANDS. YOU COULD FIND A SHIP AS WELL, AND BE BACK AT WINTERFELL WITH A MOON'S TURN, IF THE WINDS ARE KIND. BRAN AND RICKON NEED YOU.

HE WANTS ME GONE, CATELYN THOUGHT. KINGS ARE NOT SUPPOSED TO HAVE MOTHERS, AND I TELL HIM THINGS HE DOES NOT WANT TO HEAR.

MY LORD FATHER HAS LITTLE ENOUGH TIME REMAINING. SO LONG AS YOUR GRANDFATHER LIVES, MY PLACE IS AT RIVERRUN WITH HIM.

BUT I WOULD SOONER YOU SENT SOMEONE ELSE TO PYKE, AND KEPT THEON CLOSE.

THEON'S FOUGHT BRAVELY FOR US, AND I'LL HAVE NEED OF LORD GREYJOY'S LONGSHIPS.

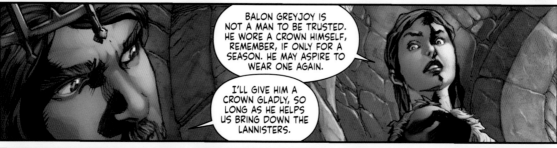

BALON GREYJOY IS NOT A MAN TO BE TRUSTED. HE WORE A CROWN HIMSELF, REMEMBER, IF ONLY FOR A SEASON. HE MAY ASPIRE TO WEAR ONE AGAIN.

I'LL GIVE HIM A CROWN GLADLY, SO LONG AS HE HELPS US BRING DOWN THE LANNISTERS.

ROBB—

I'M SENDING THEON. GOOD DAY, MOTHER. GREY WIND, COME.

I AM GOING TO VISIT FATHER. COME WITH ME, EDMURE.

I'LL VISIT HIM LATER.

THE SHORTEST WAY TO THE CENTRAL KEEP WHERE HER FATHER LAY DYING WAS THROUGH THE GODSWOOD.

A WEALTH OF LEAVES STILL CLUNG TO THE BRANCHES, IGNORANT OF THE WORD THE WHITE RAVEN HAD BROUGHT. AUTUMN HAD COME.

DOES ROBB KNOW YOU ARE RETURNED, UNCLE?

NO. I CAME HERE STRAIGHT FROM THE STABLE. HIS GRACE WILL WANT TO HEAR MY TIDINGS IN PRIVATE FIRST, I'D THINK.

HOW IS HE?

MUCH THE SAME. THE MAESTER GIVES HIM DREAMWINE AND MILK OF THE POPPY FOR HIS PAIN, SO HE SLEEPS MOST OF THE TIME.

COME OUTSIDE. BEST IF WE DO NOT WAKE HIM.

YOU CAN SEE IT BY DAY NOW. MY MEN CALL IT THE RED MESSENGER... BUT WHAT IS THE MESSAGE?

THE GREATJON TOLD ROBB THAT THE OLD GODS HAVE UNFURLED A RED FLAG OF VENGEANCE FOR NED.

EDMURE THINKS IT'S AN OMEN OF VICTORY FOR RIVERRUN—HE SEES A FISH WITH A LONG TAIL, IN THE TULLY COLORS, RED AGAINST BLUE.

I WISH I HAD THEIR FAITH. CRIMSON IS A LANNISTER COLOR.

THAT THING'S NOT CRIMSON. NOR TULLY RED. THAT'S BLOOD UP THERE, CHILD, SMEARED ACROSS THE SKY.

OUR BLOOD OR THEIRS?

WAS THERE EVER A WAR WHERE ONLY ONE SIDE BLED?

THE RIVERLANDS ARE AWASH IN BLOOD AND FLAME ALL AROUND THE GODS EYE. THE FIGHTING HAS SPREAD SOUTH TO THE BLACKWATER AND NORTH ACROSS THE TRIDENT, ALMOST TO THE TWINS.

AND TYWIN LANNISTER SITS SAFE BEHIND THE WALLS OF HARRENHAL, FEEDING HIS HOST ON OUR HARVEST AND BURNING WHAT HE DOES NOT TAKE.

GREGOR CLEGANE IS NOT THE ONLY DOG HE'S LOOSED. SER AMORY LORCH IS IN THE FIELD AS WELL, AND SOME SELLSWORD OUT OF QOHOR WHO'D SOONER MAIM A MAN THAN KILL HIM.

I'VE SEEN WHAT THEY LEAVE BEHIND. WHOLE VILLAGES PUT TO THE TORCH, WOMEN RAPED AND MURDERED, BUTCHERED CHILDREN LEFT UNBURIED TO DRAW WOLVES AND WILD DOGS...

WHEN EDMURE HEARS THIS, HE WILL RAGE.

AND THAT WILL BE JUST AS LORD TYWIN DESIRES. LANNISTER WANTS TO PROVOKE US TO BATTLE.

AND ROBB IS LIKE TO GIVE HIM THAT WISH.

HER SON HAD WON TWO GREAT VICTORIES, BUT FROM THE WAY HIS BANNERMEN SPOKE OF HIM, HE MIGHT HAVE BEEN AEGON THE CONQUEROR REBORN.

THE FIRST RULE OF WAR, CAT—NEVER GIVE THE ENEMY HIS WISH. LORD TYWIN WOULD LIKE TO FIGHT ON A FIELD OF HIS OWN CHOOSING. HE WANTS US TO MARCH ON HARRENHAL.

HARRENHAL...

EVERY CHILD KNEW THE TALES TOLD OF HARRENHAL, THE VAST FORTRESS THAT KING HARREN THE BLACK HAD RAISED BESIDE THE GODS EYE THREE HUNDRED YEARS PAST.

FORTY YEARS IT HAD TAKEN TO BUILD, AND ON THE VERY DAY KING HARREN TOOK UP RESIDENCE, AEGON THE CONQUEROR HAD COME ASHORE AT KING'S LANDING.

KING HARREN SOON LEARNED THAT THICK WALLS AND HIGH TOWERS ARE SMALL USE AGAINST DRAGONS. HARREN AND ALL HIS LINE HAD PERISHED, AND EVERY HOUSE THAT HAD HELD HARRENHAL SINCE HAD COME TO MISFORTUNE.

STRONG IT MIGHT BE, BUT IT WAS A DARK PLACE, AND CURSED.

I WOULD NOT HAVE ROBB FIGHT A BATTLE IN THE SHADOW OF THAT KEEP. WE MUST DO **SOMETHING**, UNCLE.

AND SOON. THE MEN I SENT WEST HAVE BROUGHT BACK WORD THAT A NEW HOST IS GATHERING AT CASTERLY ROCK.

YET LORD TYWIN IS NOT THE KINGSLAYER. HE WILL NOT RUSH IN HEEDLESS. HE WILL WAIT PATIENTLY FOR THIS NEW FORCE TO MARCH BEFORE HE STIRS FROM BEHIND THE WALLS OF HARRENHAL.

UNLESS...

YES?

UNLESS HE **MUST** LEAVE HARRENHAL...TO FACE SOME OTHER THREAT.

LORD RENLY.

KING RENLY.

PERHAPS. HE'LL WANT SOMETHING, THOUGH.

HE'LL WANT WHAT KINGS ALWAYS WANT...

HOMAGE.

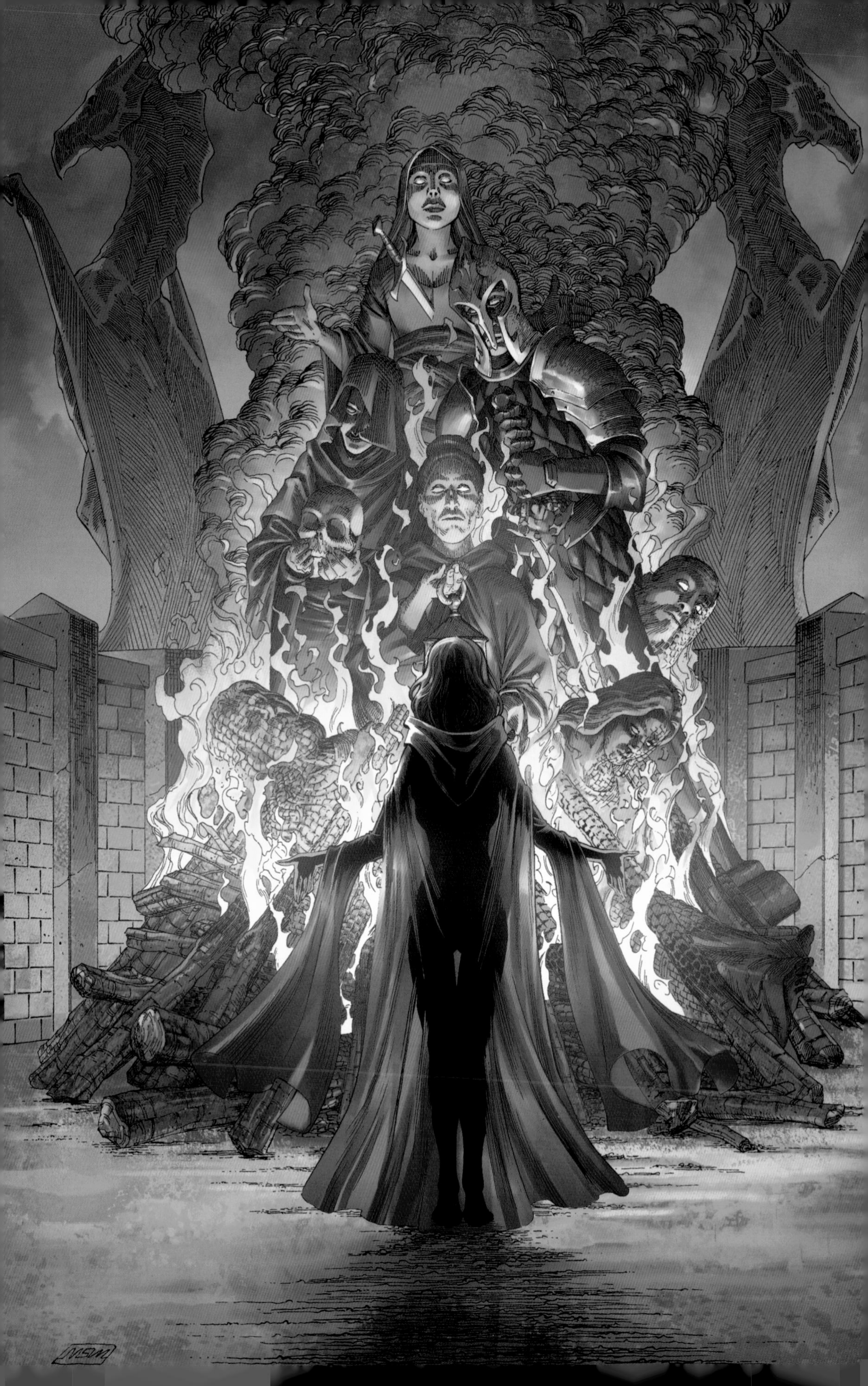

TYRION

"MORE WINE?"

JANOS SLYNT WAS A BUTCHER'S SON, AND HE LAUGHED LIKE A MAN CHOPPING MEAT.

I SHOULD NOT OBJECT. THAT'S A FINE RED. FROM THE ARBOR?

DORNISH. QUITE THE FIND. DORNISH WINES ARE NOT OFTEN SO RICH.

RICH...THE VERY WORD I WAS SEARCHING FOR. YOU HAVE A GIFT FOR WORDS, LORD TYRION.

I'M PLEASED YOU THINK SO...BUT I'M NOT A LORD, AS YOU ARE. A SIMPLE TYRION WILL SUFFICE.

YOU'RE A BOLD MAN, TO TAKE HARRENHAL FOR YOUR SEAT. SUCH A GRIM PLACE, AND COSTLY TO MAINTAIN. AND SOME SAY CURSED AS WELL.

SHOULD I FEAR A PILE OF STONE? A BOLD MAN, YOU SAID. YOU MUST BE BOLD, TO RISE AS I HAVE.

TRULY. I HAVE BEEN GLANCING OVER THE NAMES YOU PUT FORWARD TO TAKE YOUR PLACE AS COMMANDER OF THE CITY WATCH.

ANY OF THE SIX WILL DO, BUT I'D CHOOSE ALLAR DEEM. MY RIGHT ARM. GOOD MAN. LOYAL.

I HAD BEEN CONSIDERING SER JACELYN BYWATER. HE'S BEEN CAPTAIN ON THE MUD GATE FOR THREE YEARS, AND YET HIS NAME DOES NOT APPEAR ON YOUR LIST.

BYWATER. WELL. BRAVE MAN, TO BE SURE, YET THE MEN DON'T LIKE HIM. A CRIPPLE TOO. LOST HIS HAND AT PYKE DURING GREYJOY'S REBELLION; THAT'S WHAT GOT HIM KNIGHTED. A POOR TRADE, IF YOU ASK ME.

NO, SER JACELYN THINKS OVERMUCH OF HIMSELF AND HIS HONOR. ALLAR DEEM'S THE MAN FOR YOU.

YET DEEM IS LITTLE LOVED IN THE STREETS. WHAT WAS IT I HEARD OF HIM? SOME TROUBLE IN A BROTHEL?

NOT HIS FAULT, MY LO— TYRION. HE NEVER MEANT TO KILL THE WOMAN. HE WARNED HER TO STAND ASIDE AND LET HIM DO HIS DUTY.

STILL, HE MIGHT HAVE EXPECTED THE MOTHER WOULD TRY TO SAVE HER BABE. HAVE SOME OF THIS CHEESE, IT GOES SPLENDIDLY WITH THE WINE. TELL ME, WHY DID YOU CHOOSE DEEM FOR THAT UNHAPPY TASK?

A HARD MAN FOR A HARD JOB, IS DEEM. DOES AS HE'S TOLD, AND NEVER A WORD AFTERWARD.

SO WHO SENT YOU AFTER THE WHORE'S BASTARD?

IT TAKES MORE THAN WINE AND CHEESE TO MAKE JANOS SLYNT TELL MORE THAN HE SHOULD.

AS WITH DEEM. YOU MAKE HIM YOUR COMMANDER WHEN I'M OFF TO HARRENHAL, AND YOU WON'T REGRET IT.

WHOEVER THE KING NAMES WILL NOT HAVE AN EASY TIME STEPPING INTO YOUR ARMOR, I CAN TELL.

LORD MORMONT FACES THE SAME PROBLEM. THE WATCH GETS SO FEW GOOD MEN THESE DAYS. HE'D SLEEP EASIER IF HE HAD A MAN LIKE YOU, I IMAGINE. OR THE VALIANT ALLAR DEEM.

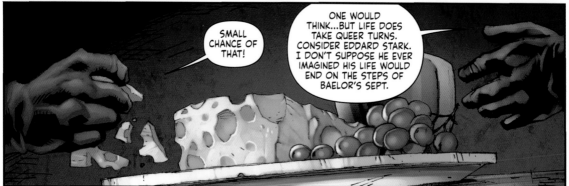

SMALL CHANCE OF THAT!

ONE WOULD THINK...BUT LIFE DOES TAKE QUEER TURNS. CONSIDER EDDARD STARK. I DON'T SUPPOSE HE EVER IMAGINED HIS LIFE WOULD END ON THE STEPS OF BAELOR'S SEPT.

YES. AS TO THAT, WELL...THE KING COMMANDED IT, M'LORD.

THE KING IS THIRTEEN.

STILL, HE IS THE KING. THE LORD OF THE SEVEN KINGDOMS.

WELL, ONE OR TWO OF THEM, AT LEAST. TELL ME, MY LORD, DID YOU DRIVE THE SPEAR INTO THE MAN'S BACK YOURSELF, OR DID YOU ONLY GIVE THE COMMAND?

I GAVE THE COMMAND, AND I'D GIVE IT AGAIN! LORD STARK WAS A TRAITOR. THE MAN TRIED TO BUY ME.

LITTLE DREAMING THAT YOU HAD ALREADY BEEN SOLD.

ARE YOU DRUNK? IF YOU THINK I WILL SIT HERE AND HAVE MY HONOR QUESTIONED—

WHAT HONOR? I ADMIT, YOU MADE A BETTER BARGAIN THAN SER JACELYN. A LORDSHIP *AND* A CASTLE FOR A SPEAR THRUST IN THE BACK, AND YOU DIDN'T EVEN NEED TO THRUST THE SPEAR.

I MISLIKE THE TONE OF YOUR VOICE, MY LO—*IMP*. I AM THE LORD OF HARRENHAL AND A MEMBER OF THE KING'S COUNCIL. WHO ARE YOU TO CHASTISE ME LIKE THIS?

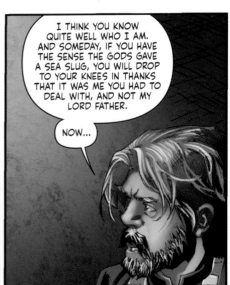

I THINK YOU KNOW QUITE WELL WHO I AM. AND SOMEDAY, IF YOU HAVE THE SENSE THE GODS GAVE A SEA SLUG, YOU WILL DROP TO YOUR KNEES IN THANKS THAT IT WAS ME YOU HAD TO DEAL WITH, AND NOT MY LORD FATHER.

NOW...

JANOS.

LORD SLYNT, I BELIEVE YOU KNOW SER JACELYN BYWATER, OUR NEW COMMANDER OF THE CITY WATCH.

WE HAVE A LITTER WAITING FOR YOU, MY LORD. THE DOCKS ARE DARK AND DISTANT, AND THE STREETS ARE NOT SAFE BY NIGHT.

WH-WHAT...WHAT DO YOU...?

MEAN TO DO WITH YOU? THE CARRACK *SUMMER'S DREAM* SAILS ON THE MORNING TIDE. WHEN YOU SEE LORD COMMANDER MORMONT, GIVE HIM MY FOND REGARDS, AND TELL HIM THAT I HAVE NOT FORGOTTEN THE NEEDS OF THE NIGHT'S WATCH.

I WISH YOU LONG LIFE AND GOOD SERVICE, MY LORD.

IT'S A LONG VOYAGE, AND LORD SLYNT WILL WANT FOR COMPANY. SEE THAT THESE SIX JOIN HIM ON THE *SUMMER'S DREAM*.

THERE'S ONE... DEEM. TELL THE CAPTAIN IT WOULD NOT BE TAKEN AMISS IF THAT ONE SHOULD HAPPEN TO BE SWEPT OVERBOARD BEFORE THEY REACH EASTWATCH-BY-THE-SEA.

I'M TOLD THOSE NORTHERN WATERS ARE VERY STORMY, MY LORD.

OH, SWEETLY DONE, MY GOOD LORD.

THEN WHY DO I HAVE THIS BITTER TASTE IN MY MOUTH?

I TOLD THEM TO THROW ALLAR DEEM INTO THE SEA. I AM SORELY TEMPTED TO DO THE SAME WITH YOU.

YOU MIGHT BE DISAPPOINTED BY THE RESULT. THE STORMS COME AND GO, AND I KEEP ON PADDLING. MIGHT I TROUBLE YOU FOR A TASTE OF THE WINE THAT LORD SLYNT ENJOYED SO MUCH?

AH. SWEET AS SUMMER. I HEAR THE GRAPES SINGING ON MY TONGUE.

I WONDERED WHAT THAT NOISE WAS. TELL THE GRAPES TO KEEP STILL, MY HEAD IS ABOUT TO SPLIT.

IT WAS MY SISTER. THAT WAS WHAT THE OH-SO-LOYAL LORD JANOS REFUSED TO SAY. CERSEI SENT THE GOLD CLOAKS TO THAT BROTHEL.

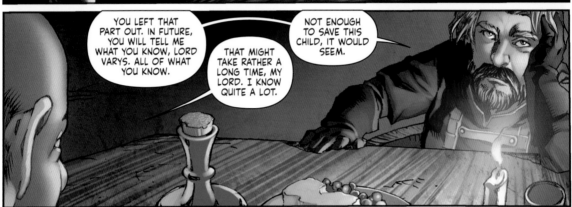

YOU LEFT THAT PART OUT. IN FUTURE, YOU WILL TELL ME WHAT YOU KNOW, LORD VARYS. ALL OF WHAT YOU KNOW.

THAT MIGHT TAKE RATHER A LONG TIME, MY LORD. I KNOW QUITE A LOT.

NOT ENOUGH TO SAVE THIS CHILD, IT WOULD SEEM.

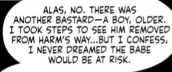

ALAS, NO. THERE WAS ANOTHER BASTARD—A BOY, OLDER. I TOOK STEPS TO SEE HIM REMOVED FROM HARM'S WAY...BUT I CONFESS, I NEVER DREAMED THE BABE WOULD BE AT RISK.

A BASEBORN GIRL, LESS THAN A YEAR OLD, WITH A WHORE FOR A MOTHER. WHAT THREAT COULD SHE POSE?

SHE WAS ROBERT'S. THAT WAS ENOUGH FOR CERSEI, IT WOULD SEEM.

IT IS GRIEVOUS SAD. THE POOR SWEET BABE AND HER MOTHER, WHO WAS SO YOUNG AND LOVED THE KING.

TYRION HAD NEVER SEEN THE DEAD GIRL'S FACE, BUT IN HIS MIND SHE WAS SHAE AND TYSHA, BOTH.

CAN A WHORE TRULY LOVE ANYONE, I WONDER? NO, DON'T ANSWER. SOME THINGS I WOULD RATHER NOT KNOW.

YET IT DOES SEEM MY SISTER WAS TELLING THE TRUTH ABOUT STARK'S DEATH. WE HAVE MY NEPHEW TO THANK FOR THAT MADNESS.

WITH THE CITY WATCH IN HAND, MY LORD, YOU ARE WELL PLACED TO SEE TO IT THAT HIS GRACE COMMITS NO FURTHER...FOLLIES. YOU WILL FIND SER JACELYN TO BE COURAGEOUS, HONORABLE, OBEDIENT...AND MOST GRATEFUL.

TO WHOM, I WONDER? WHY ARE YOU SO HELPFUL, MY LORD VARYS?

YOU ARE THE HAND. I SERVE THE REALM, THE KING, AND YOU.

AS YOU SERVED JON ARRYN AND EDDARD STARK?

I SERVED LORD ARRYN AND LORD STARK AS BEST I COULD. I WAS SADDENED AND HORRIFIED BY THEIR MOST UNTIMELY DEATHS.

THINK HOW *I* FEEL. I'M LIKE TO BE NEXT.

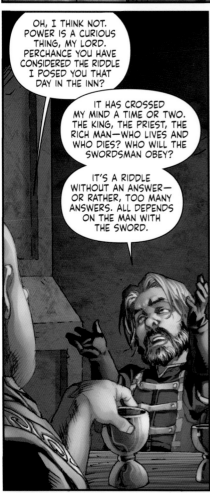

OH, I THINK NOT. POWER IS A CURIOUS THING, MY LORD. PERCHANCE YOU HAVE CONSIDERED THE RIDDLE I POSED YOU THAT DAY IN THE INN?

IT HAS CROSSED MY MIND A TIME OR TWO. THE KING, THE PRIEST, THE RICH MAN—WHO LIVES AND WHO DIES? WHO WILL THE SWORDSMAN OBEY?

IT'S A RIDDLE WITHOUT AN ANSWER— OR RATHER, TOO MANY ANSWERS. ALL DEPENDS ON THE MAN WITH THE SWORD.

AND YET HE IS NO ONE. HE HAS NEITHER CROWN NOR GOLD NOR FAVOR OF THE GODS, ONLY A PIECE OF POINTED STEEL.

THAT PIECE OF STEEL IS THE POWER OF LIFE AND DEATH.

JUST SO...YET WHY THEN DO WE PRETEND OUR KINGS HOLD THE POWER? WHY SHOULD A STRONG MAN WITH A SWORD EVER OBEY A CHILD KING LIKE JOFFREY, OR A WINE-SODDEN OAF LIKE HIS FATHER?

BECAUSE THESE CHILD KINGS AND DRUNKEN OAFS CAN CALL OTHER STRONG MEN, WITH OTHER SWORDS.

THEN THESE OTHER SWORDSMEN HAVE THE TRUE POWER. OR DO THEY?

DID YOU MEAN TO ANSWER YOUR DAMNED RIDDLE, OR ONLY TO MAKE MY HEAD ACHE WORSE?

HERE, THEN. POWER RESIDES WHERE MEN BELIEVE IT RESIDES. NO MORE AND NO LESS.

SO POWER IS A MUMMER'S TRICK?

A SHADOW ON THE WALL. YET SHADOWS CAN KILL. AND OFTTIMES A VERY SMALL MAN CAN CAST A VERY LARGE SHADOW.

LORD VARYS, I AM GROWING STRANGELY FOND OF YOU. I MAY KILL YOU YET, BUT I THINK I'D FEEL SAD ABOUT IT.

WHAT ARE YOU, VARYS? A SPIDER, THEY SAY.

SPIES AND INFORMERS ARE SELDOM LOVED, MY LORD. I AM BUT A LOYAL SERVANT OF THE REALM.

AND A EUNUCH. LET US NOT FORGET THAT.

I SELDOM DO.

PEOPLE HAVE CALLED ME A HALFMAN TOO, YET I'M STILL A MAN. WHO CUT YOU, VARYS? WHEN AND WHY?

YOU ARE KIND TO ASK, MY LORD, BUT MY TALE IS LONG AND SAD, AND WE BOTH HAVE MUCH TO DO.

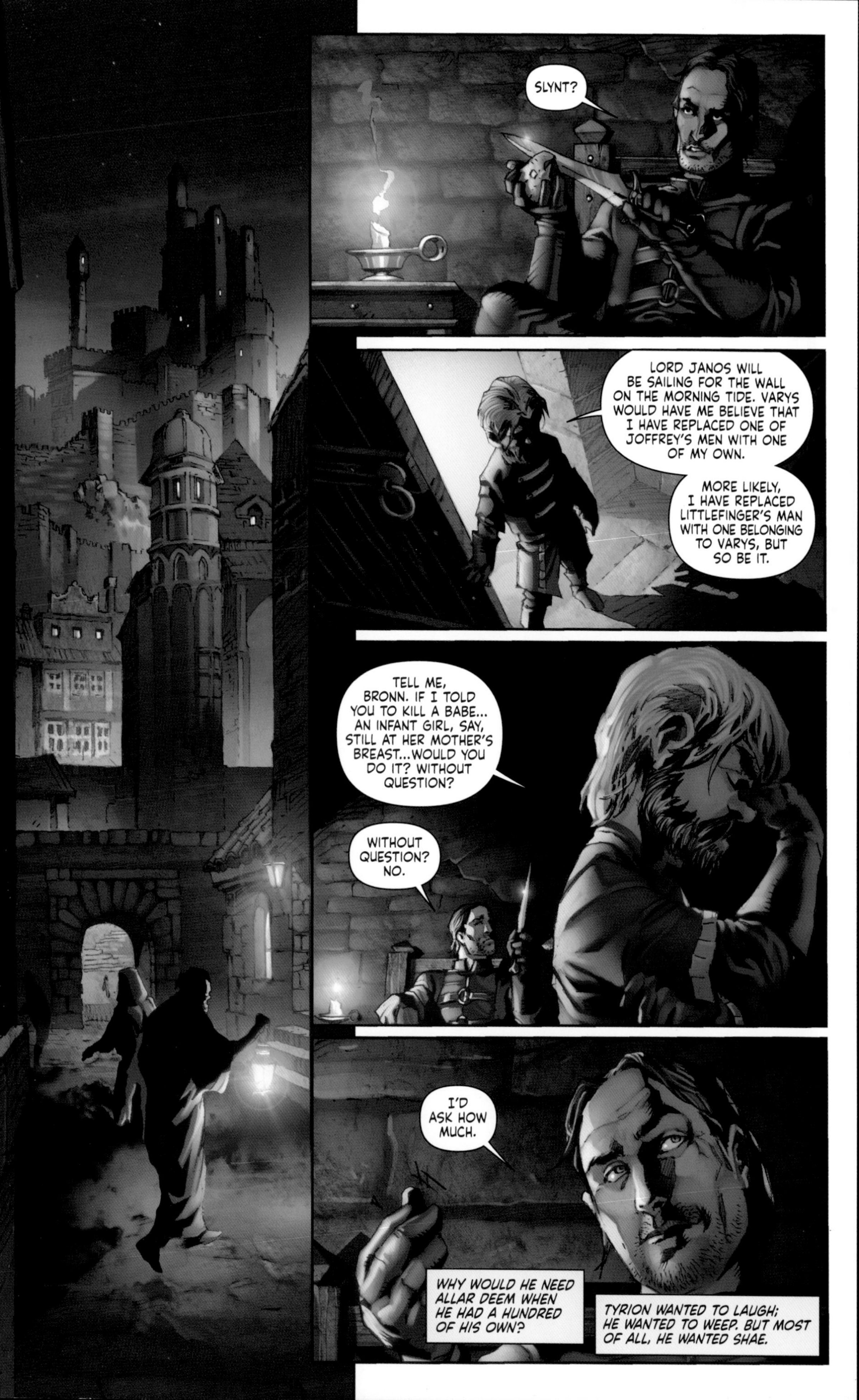
SLYNT?
LORD JANOS WILL BE SAILING FOR THE WALL ON THE MORNING TIDE. VARYS WOULD HAVE ME BELIEVE THAT I HAVE REPLACED ONE OF JOFFREY'S MEN WITH ONE OF MY OWN.
MORE LIKELY, I HAVE REPLACED LITTLEFINGER'S MAN WITH ONE BELONGING TO VARYS, BUT SO BE IT.
TELL ME, BRONN. IF I TOLD YOU TO KILL A BABE... AN INFANT GIRL, SAY, STILL AT HER MOTHER'S BREAST...WOULD YOU DO IT? WITHOUT QUESTION?
WITHOUT QUESTION? NO.
I'D ASK HOW MUCH.
WHY WOULD HE NEED ALLAR DEEM WHEN HE HAD A HUNDRED OF HIS OWN?
TYRION WANTED TO LAUGH; HE WANTED TO WEEP. BUT MOST OF ALL, HE WANTED SHAE.

DAVOS

THE MORNING AIR WAS DARK WITH THE SMOKE OF BURNING GODS.

DRAGONSTONE'S SEPT HAD BEEN WHERE AEGON THE CONQUEROR KNELT TO PRAY THE NIGHT BEFORE HE SAILED.

THAT HAD NOT SAVED IT FROM THE QUEEN'S MEN.

THEY HAD OVERTURNED THE ALTARS, PULLED DOWN THE STATUES, AND SMASHED THE STAINED GLASS WITH WARHAMMERS.

AN ILL THING.

SEPTON BARRE COULD ONLY CURSE THEM, BUT SER HUBARD RAMBTON LED HIS THREE SONS TO THE SEPT TO DEFEND THEIR GODS.

THE RAMBTONS HAD SLAIN FOUR OF THE QUEEN'S MEN BEFORE THE OTHERS OVERWHELMED THEM.

AFTERWARD GUNCER SUNGLASS, MILDEST AND MOST PIOUS OF LORDS, TOLD STANNIS HE COULD NO LONGER SUPPORT HIS CLAIM.

NOW HE SHARED A SWELTERING CELL WITH THE SEPTON AND SER HUBARD'S TWO SURVIVING SONS.

SILENCE, ALLARD.

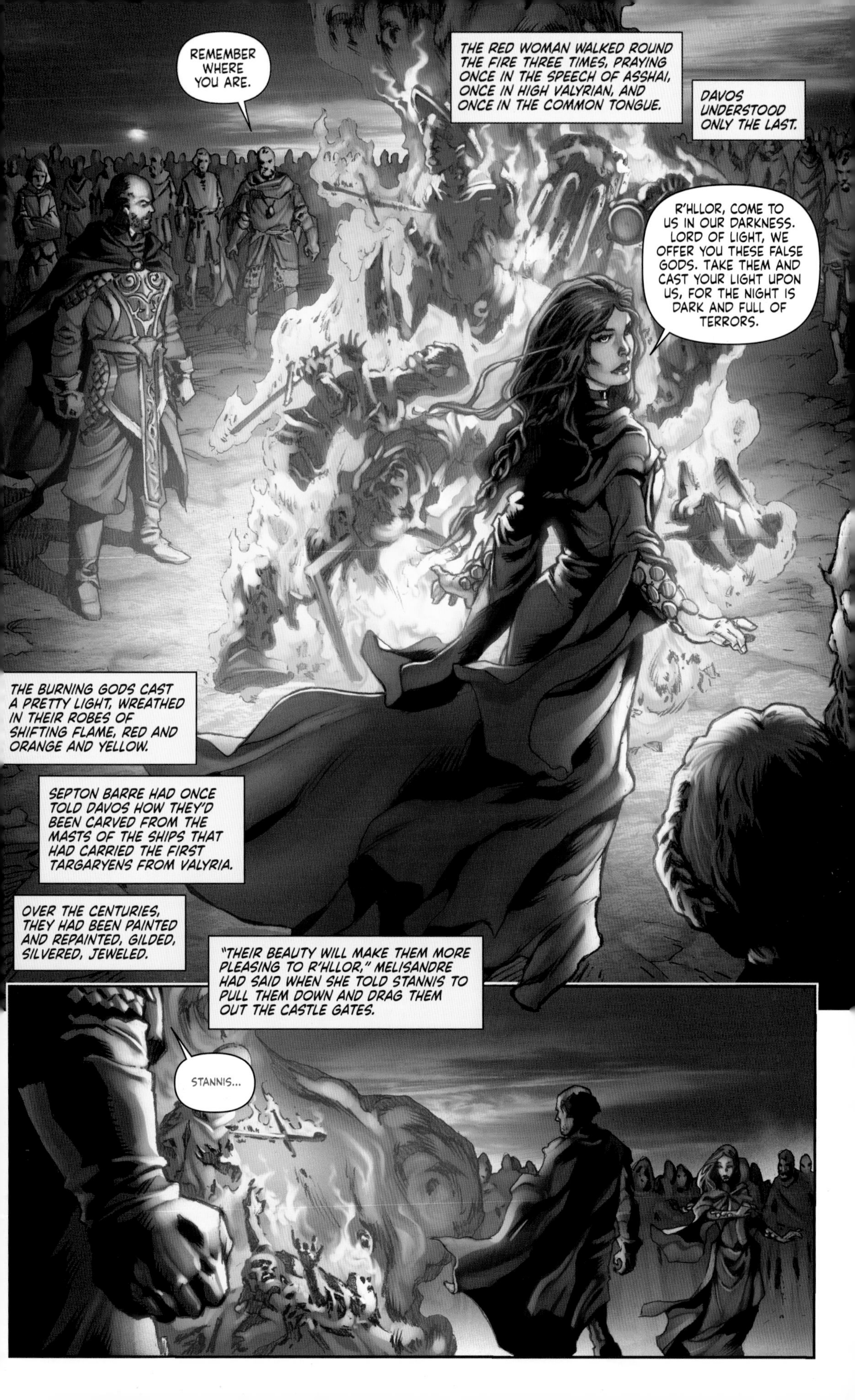
REMEMBER WHERE YOU ARE.
THE RED WOMAN WALKED ROUND THE FIRE THREE TIMES, PRAYING ONCE IN THE SPEECH OF ASSHAI, ONCE IN HIGH VALYRIAN, AND ONCE IN THE COMMON TONGUE.
DAVOS UNDERSTOOD ONLY THE LAST.
R'HLLOR, COME TO US IN OUR DARKNESS. LORD OF LIGHT, WE OFFER YOU THESE FALSE GODS. TAKE THEM AND CAST YOUR LIGHT UPON US, FOR THE NIGHT IS DARK AND FULL OF TERRORS.
THE BURNING GODS CAST A PRETTY LIGHT, WREATHED IN THEIR ROBES OF SHIFTING FLAME, RED AND ORANGE AND YELLOW.
SEPTON BARRE HAD ONCE TOLD DAVOS HOW THEY'D BEEN CARVED FROM THE MASTS OF THE SHIPS THAT HAD CARRIED THE FIRST TARGARYENS FROM VALYRIA.
OVER THE CENTURIES, THEY HAD BEEN PAINTED AND REPAINTED, GILDED, SILVERED, JEWELED.
"THEIR BEAUTY WILL MAKE THEM MORE PLEASING TO R'HLLOR," MELISANDRE HAD SAID WHEN SHE TOLD STANNIS TO PULL THEM DOWN AND DRAG THEM OUT THE CASTLE GATES.
STANNIS...

STANNIS HAD RAISED DAVOS TO KNIGHTHOOD. HE HAD GIVEN HIM A PLACE OF HONOR AT HIS TABLE, A WAR GALLEY TO SAIL IN PLACE OF A SMUGGLER'S SKIFF.

...EVERYTHING I AM, I OWE TO HIM.

HIS SONS HAD RISEN AS WELL. DALE AND ALLARD CAPTAINED GALLEYS, MARIC WAS OARMASTER ON THE *FURY*, MATTHOS SERVED HIS FATHER ON *BLACK BETHA*, AND THE KING HAD TAKEN DEVAN AS A ROYAL SQUIRE.

ONE DAY DEVAN WOULD BE KNIGHTED, AND THE TWO LITTLE LADS AS WELL. MARYA WAS MISTRESS OF A SMALL KEEP ON CAPE WRATH, WITH SERVANTS WHO CALLED HER M'LADY, AND DAVOS COULD HUNT RED DEER IN HIS OWN WOODS.

ALL THIS HE HAD OF STANNIS BARATHEON, FOR THE PRICE OF A FEW FINGER JOINTS.

IN ANCIENT BOOKS OF ASSHAI IT IS WRITTEN THAT THERE WILL COME A DAY AFTER A LONG SUMMER WHEN THE STARS BLEED AND THE COLD BREATH OF DARKNESS FALLS HEAVY ON THE WORLD.

IN THIS DREAD HOUR A WARRIOR SHALL DRAW FROM THE FIRE A BURNING SWORD.

AND THAT SWORD SHALL BE LIGHTBRINGER, THE RED SWORD OF HEROES, AND HE WHO CLASPS IT SHALL BE AZOR AHAI COME AGAIN, AND THE DARKNESS SHALL FLEE BEFORE HIM.

AZOR AHAI, BELOVED OF R'HLLOR! THE WARRIOR OF LIGHT, THE SON OF FIRE! COME FORTH, YOUR SWORD AWAITS YOU!

UNDER THE SEA, SMOKE RISES IN BUBBLES, AND FLAMES BURN GREEN AND BLUE AND BLACK.

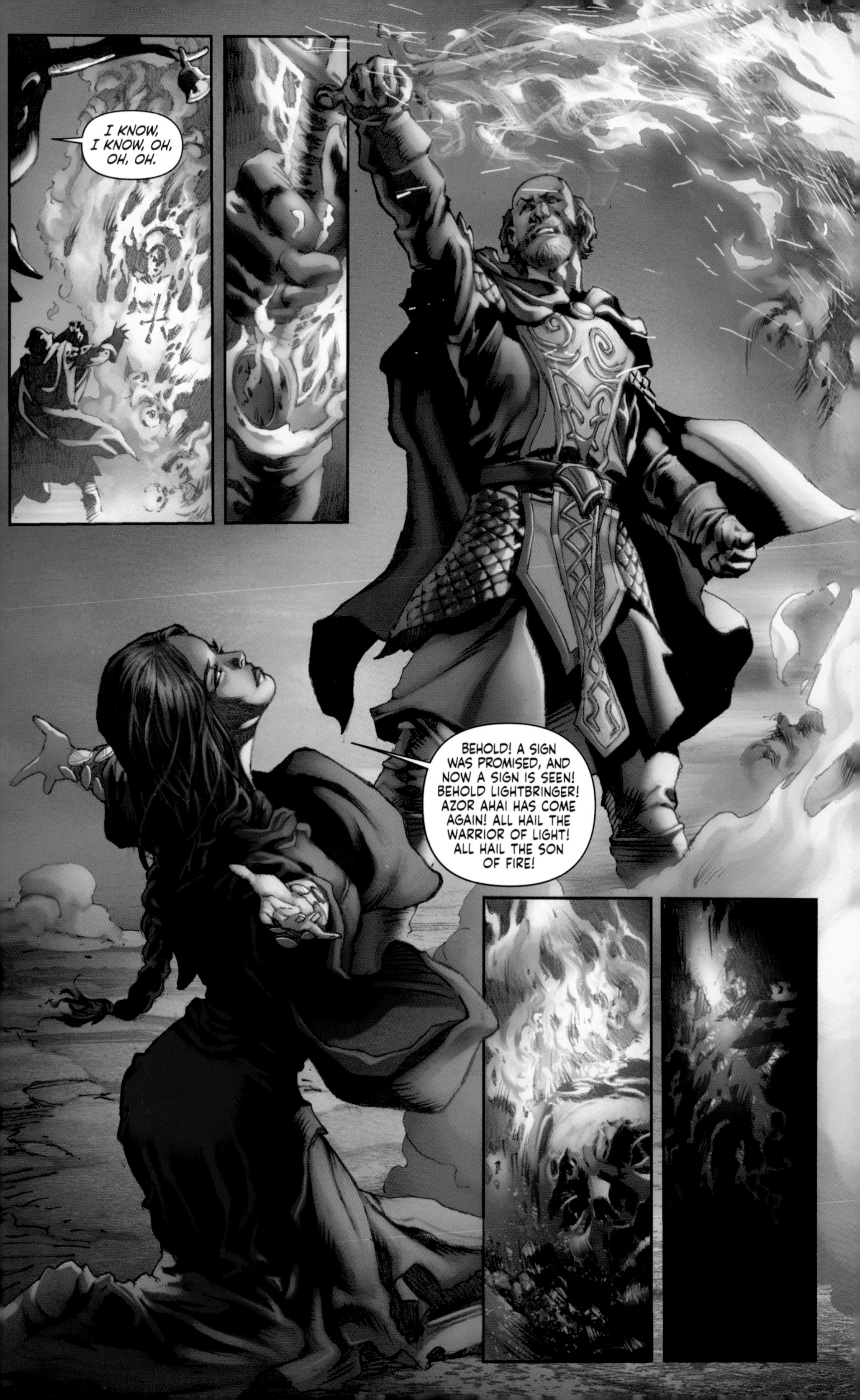
I KNOW, I KNOW, OH, OH, OH.
BEHOLD! A SIGN WAS PROMISED, AND NOW A SIGN IS SEEN! BEHOLD LIGHTBRINGER! AZOR AHAI HAS COME AGAIN! ALL HAIL THE WARRIOR OF LIGHT! ALL HAIL THE SON OF FIRE!

"SER KNIGHT, COME SIT WITH ME. EAT A GRAPE. EAT TWO. THEY ARE MARVELOUSLY SWEET."

SALLADHOR SAAN, OLD FRIEND.

IT'S ALE I NEED, AND NEWS. HOW WELL IS THE CITY DEFENDED?

THE MEN OF WESTEROS ARE EVER RUSHING. WHAT GOOD IS THIS, I ASK YOU?

THE LORD OF CASTERLY ROCK HAS SENT HIS DWARF TO SEE TO KING'S LANDING. PERHAPS HE HOPES THAT HIS UGLY FACE WILL FRIGHTEN OFF ATTACKERS, EH?

THE DWARF HAS CHASED OFF THE LOUT WHO RULED THE GOLD CLOAKS AND PUT IN HIS PLACE A KNIGHT WITH AN IRON HAND.

THE WALLS ARE HIGH AND STRONG, BUT WHO WILL MAN THEM? THEY ARE BUILDING SCORPIONS AND SPITFIRES, OH, YES, BUT THE MEN IN THE GOLDEN CLOAKS ARE TOO FEW AND TOO GREEN, AND THERE ARE NO OTHERS.

A SWIFT STRIKE, LIKE A HAWK PLUMMETING AT A HARE, AND THE GREAT CITY WILL BE OURS. GRANT US WIND TO FILL OUR SAILS, AND YOUR KING COULD SIT UPON HIS IRON THRONE BY EVEN-FALL ON THE MORROW.

EVEN THESE GRAPES COULD BE NO MORE RIPE THAN THAT CITY, MY OLD FRIEND.

MIGHT BE WE COULD TAKE KING'S LANDING, BUT HOW LONG WOULD WE HOLD IT? TYWIN LANNISTER IS KNOWN TO BE AT HARRENHAL WITH A GREAT HOST, AND LORD RENLY...

AH, YES, THE YOUNG BROTHER. THAT PART IS NOT SO GOOD, MY FRIEND. KING RENLY BESTIRS HIMSELF. NO, HERE HE IS LORD RENLY, MY PARDONS. SO MANY KINGS, MY TONGUE GROWS WEARY OF THE WORD.

THE BROTHER RENLY HAS LEFT HIGHGARDEN WITH HIS FAIR YOUNG QUEEN, HIS FLOWERED LORDS AND SHINING KNIGHTS, AND A MIGHTY HOST OF FOOT.

HE MARCHES UP YOUR ROAD OF ROSES TOWARD THE VERY SAME GREAT CITY WE WERE SPEAKING OF.

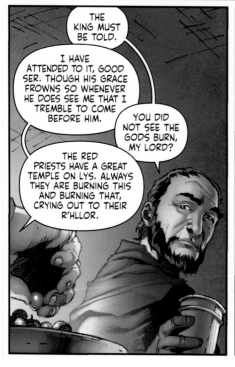

THE KING MUST BE TOLD.

I HAVE ATTENDED TO IT, GOOD SER. THOUGH HIS GRACE FROWNS SO WHENEVER HE DOES SEE ME THAT I TREMBLE TO COME BEFORE HIM.

YOU DID NOT SEE THE GODS BURN, MY LORD?

THE RED PRIESTS HAVE A GREAT TEMPLE ON LYS. ALWAYS THEY ARE BURNING THIS AND BURNING THAT, CRYING OUT TO THEIR R'HLLOR.

THEY BORE ME WITH THEIR FIRES. SOON THEY WILL BORE KING STANNIS TOO, IT IS TO BE HOPED.

DO YOU KNOW THE TALE OF THE FORGING OF LIGHTBRINGER? I SHALL TELL IT TO YOU.

IT WAS A TIME WHEN DARKNESS LAY HEAVY ON THE WORLD...

"TO OPPOSE THE DARKNESS, THE HERO MUST HAVE A HERO'S BLADE, OH, LIKE NONE THAT HAD EVER BEEN.

"AZOR AHAI CAPTURED A LION, TO TEMPER THE BLADE BY PLUNGING IT THROUGH THE BEAST'S RED HEART, BUT ONCE MORE THE STEEL SHATTERED AND SPLIT.

"AND SO FOR THIRTY DAYS AND THIRTY NIGHTS AZOR AHAI LABORED SLEEPLESS IN THE TEMPLE, FORGING A BLADE IN THE SACRED FIRES. YET WHEN HE PLUNGED IT INTO WATER TO TEMPER THE STEEL IT BURST ASUNDER.

"GREAT WAS HIS WOE AND GREAT WAS HIS SORROW THEN, FOR HE KNEW WHAT HE MUST DO.

"AGAIN HE BEGAN. THE SECOND TIME IT TOOK HIM FIFTY DAYS AND FIFTY NIGHTS, AND THIS SWORD SEEMED EVEN FINER THAN THE FIRST.

"A HUNDRED DAYS AND A HUNDRED NIGHTS HE LABORED ON THE THIRD BLADE, AND AS IT GLOWED WHITE-HOT IN THE SACRED FIRES, HE SUMMONED HIS WIFE.

"*NISSA NISSA,*' HE SAID TO HER, FOR THAT WAS HER NAME, '*BARE YOUR BREAST, AND KNOW THAT I LOVE YOU BEST OF ALL THAT IS IN THIS WORLD.*'

"SHE DID THIS THING, WHY I CANNOT SAY, AND AZOR AHAI THRUST THE SMOKING SWORD THROUGH HER LIVING HEART.

"IT IS SAID THAT HER CRY OF ANGUISH AND ECSTASY LEFT A CRACK ACROSS THE FACE OF THE MOON, BUT HER BLOOD AND HER SOUL AND HER STRENGTH AND HER COURAGE ALL WENT INTO THE STEEL.

"SUCH IS THE TALE OF THE FORGING OF LIGHTBRINGER, THE RED SWORD OF HEROES."

THAT SWORD YOU SAW TODAY WAS NOT LIGHTBRINGER, MY FRIEND. BE GLAD IT IS JUST A BURNT SWORD THAT HIS GRACE PULLED FROM THAT FIRE.

TOO MUCH LIGHT CAN HURT THE EYES, MY FRIEND, AND FIRE BURNS.

"SER DAVOS, COME HAVE A LOOK AT THIS LETTER."

IT LOOKS HANDSOME ENOUGH, YOUR GRACE, BUT I FEAR I CANNOT READ THE WORDS.

I'D FORGOTTEN. PYLOS, READ IT TO HIM.

YOUR GRACE.

"ALL MEN KNOW ME FOR THE TRUEBORN SON OF STEFFON BARATHEON, LORD OF STORM'S END, BY HIS LADY WIFE CASSANA OF HOUSE ESTERMONT.

"I DECLARE UPON THE HONOR OF MY HOUSE THAT MY BELOVED BROTHER ROBERT, OUR LATE KING, LEFT NO TRUEBORN ISSUE OF HIS BODY...

"...THE BOY JOFFREY, THE BOY TOMMEN, AND THE GIRL MYRCELLA BEING ABOMINATIONS BORN OF INCEST BETWEEN CERSEI LANNISTER AND HER BROTHER JAIME THE KINGSLAYER.

"BY RIGHT OF BIRTH AND BLOOD, I DO THIS DAY LAY CLAIM TO THE IRON THRONE OF THE SEVEN KINGDOMS OF WESTEROS. LET ALL TRUE MEN DECLARE THEIR LOYALTY.

"DONE IN THE LIGHT OF THE LORD, UNDER THE SIGN AND SEAL OF STANNIS OF HOUSE BARATHEON, THE FIRST OF HIS NAME, KING OF THE ANDALS, THE RHOYNAR, AND THE FIRST MEN, AND LORD OF THE SEVEN KINGDOMS."

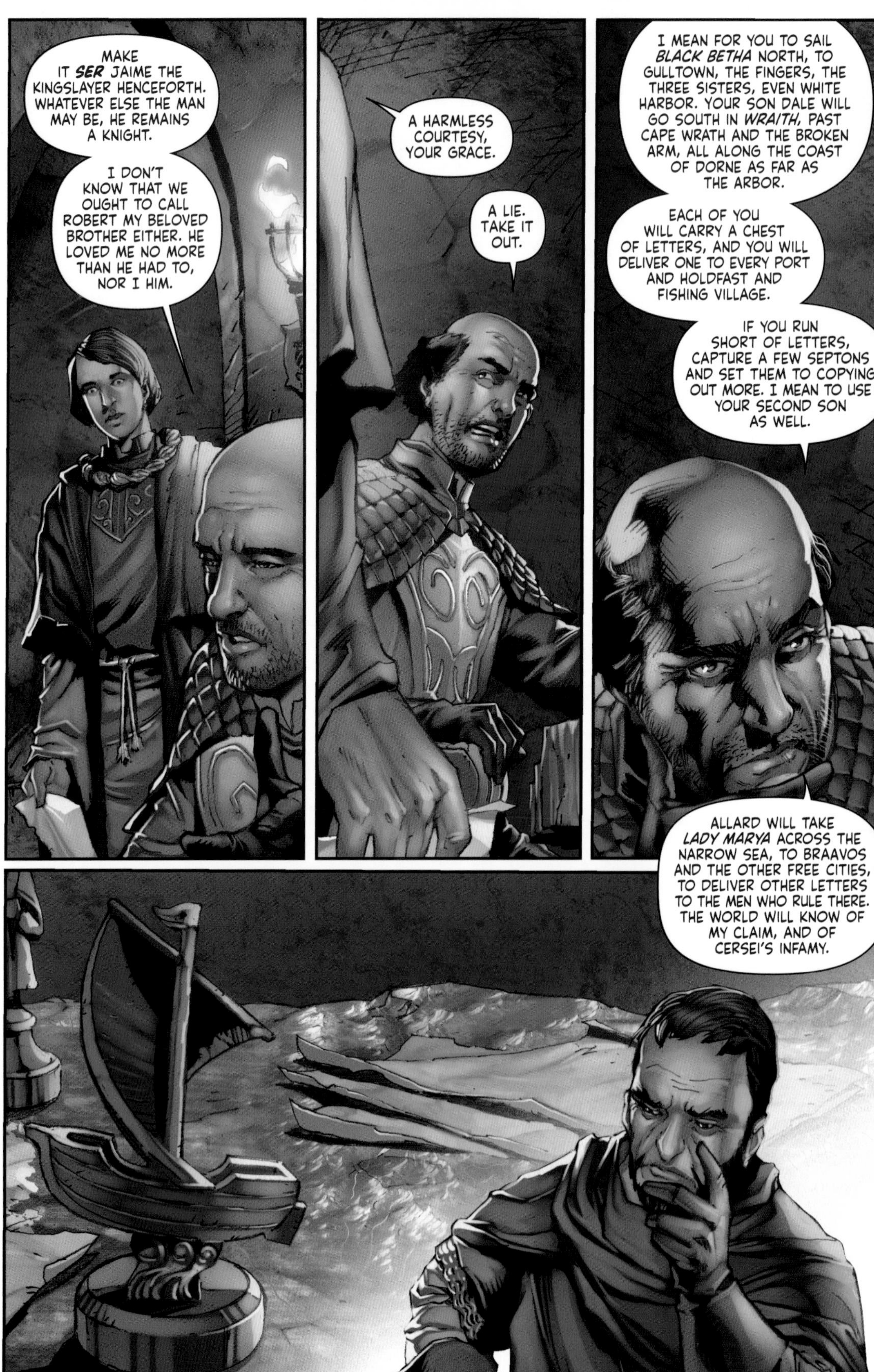
MAKE IT *SER* JAIME THE KINGSLAYER HENCEFORTH. WHATEVER ELSE THE MAN MAY BE, HE REMAINS A KNIGHT.
I DON'T KNOW THAT WE OUGHT TO CALL ROBERT MY BELOVED BROTHER EITHER. HE LOVED ME NO MORE THAN HE HAD TO, NOR I HIM.
A HARMLESS COURTESY, YOUR GRACE.
A LIE. TAKE IT OUT.
I MEAN FOR YOU TO SAIL *BLACK BETHA* NORTH, TO GULLTOWN, THE FINGERS, THE THREE SISTERS, EVEN WHITE HARBOR. YOUR SON DALE WILL GO SOUTH IN *WRAITH,* PAST CAPE WRATH AND THE BROKEN ARM, ALL ALONG THE COAST OF DORNE AS FAR AS THE ARBOR.
EACH OF YOU WILL CARRY A CHEST OF LETTERS, AND YOU WILL DELIVER ONE TO EVERY PORT AND HOLDFAST AND FISHING VILLAGE.
IF YOU RUN SHORT OF LETTERS, CAPTURE A FEW SEPTONS AND SET THEM TO COPYING OUT MORE. I MEAN TO USE YOUR SECOND SON AS WELL.
ALLARD WILL TAKE *LADY MARYA* ACROSS THE NARROW SEA, TO BRAAVOS AND THE OTHER FREE CITIES, TO DELIVER OTHER LETTERS TO THE MEN WHO RULE THERE. THE WORLD WILL KNOW OF MY CLAIM, AND OF CERSEI'S INFAMY.

MAESTER, PERHAPS YOU OUGHT GET TO YOUR WRITING. WE WILL NEED A GREAT MANY LETTERS, AND SOON.

AS YOU WILL.

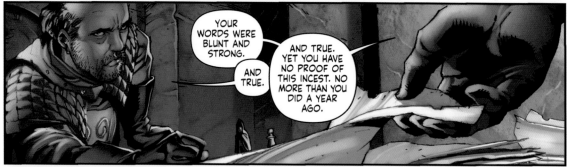

WHAT IS IT YOU WOULD NOT SAY IN THE PRESENCE OF MY MAESTER, DAVOS?

MY LIEGE... THE LETTER... WHAT DID YOUR LORDS MAKE OF IT?

CELTIGAR PRONOUNCED IT ADMIRABLE. IF I SHOWED HIM THE CONTENTS OF MY PRIVY, HE WOULD DECLARE THAT ADMIRABLE AS WELL.

THE OTHERS BOBBED THEIR HEADS UP AND DOWN LIKE A FLOCK OF GEESE—ALL BUT VELARYON, WHO SAID THAT STEEL WOULD DECIDE THE MATTER, NOT WORDS ON PARCHMENT.

I'LL HEAR YOUR VIEWS.

YOUR WORDS WERE BLUNT AND STRONG.

AND TRUE.

AND TRUE. YET YOU HAVE NO PROOF OF THIS INCEST. NO MORE THAN YOU DID A YEAR AGO.

THERE'S PROOF OF A SORT AT STORM'S END. ROBERT'S BASTARD. THE ONE HE FATHERED ON MY WEDDING NIGHT, IN THE VERY BED THEY'D MADE UP FOR ME AND MY BRIDE.

DELENA WAS A FLORENT, AND A MAIDEN WHEN HE TOOK HER, SO ROBERT ACKNOWLEDGED THE BABE. EDRIC STORM, THEY CALL HIM. HE IS SAID TO BE THE VERY IMAGE OF MY BROTHER.

IF MEN WERE TO SEE HIM, AND THEN LOOK AGAIN AT JOFFREY AND TOMMEN, THEY COULD NOT HELP BUT WONDER, I WOULD THINK.

HAVE YOU GONE DEVOUT ON ME, SMUGGLER?

I DO NOT KNOW THIS LORD OF LIGHT, BUT I KNEW THE GODS WE BURNED THIS MORNING.

THE SMITH HAS KEPT MY SHIPS SAFE, WHILE THE MOTHER HAS GIVEN ME SEVEN STRONG SONS.

THERE WAS A PHRASE AT THE END. HOW DID IT GO? DONE IN THE LIGHT OF THE LORD... YOUR PEOPLE WILL MISLIKE THOSE WORDS.

YOUR WIFE HAS GIVEN YOU SEVEN STRONG SONS. DO YOU PRAY TO HER? IT WAS WOOD WE BURNED THIS MORNING.

YOUR PEOPLE WILL NOT LOVE YOU IF YOU TAKE FROM THEM THE GODS THEY HAVE ALWAYS WORSHIPED, AND GIVE THEM ONE WHOSE VERY NAME SOUNDS QUEER ON THEIR TONGUES.

R'HLLOR. WHY IS THAT SO HARD? THEY WILL NOT LOVE ME, YOU SAY? WHEN HAVE THEY EVER LOVED ME? HOW CAN I LOSE SOMETHING I HAVE NEVER OWNED?

I STOPPED BELIEVING IN GODS THE DAY I SAW THE *WINDPROUD* BREAK UP ACROSS THE BAY. ANY GODS SO MONSTROUS AS TO DROWN MY MOTHER AND FATHER WOULD NEVER HAVE MY WORSHIP, I VOWED.

IF YOU DO NOT BELIEVE IN GODS—

—WHY TROUBLE WITH THIS NEW ONE? I HAVE ASKED MYSELF AS WELL. I KNOW LITTLE AND CARE LESS OF GODS, BUT THE RED PRIESTESS HAS POWER.

THE IRON THRONE IS MINE BY RIGHTS, BUT HOW AM I TO TAKE IT? THERE ARE FOUR KINGS IN THE REALM, AND THREE OF THEM HAVE MORE MEN AND MORE GOLD THAN I DO. I HAVE SHIPS... AND I HAVE *HER.*

THE RED WOMAN. HALF MY KNIGHTS ARE AFRAID EVEN TO SAY HER NAME, DID YOU KNOW?

IF SHE CAN DO NOTHING ELSE, A SORCERESS WHO CAN INSPIRE SUCH DREAD IN GROWN MEN IS NOT TO BE DESPISED. AND PERHAPS SHE CAN DO MORE.

WHEN I WAS A LAD I FOUND AN INJURED GOSHAWK AND NURSED HER BACK TO HEALTH. PROUDWING, I NAMED HER.

SHE WOULD PERCH ON MY SHOULDER AND FLUTTER FROM ROOM TO ROOM AFTER ME AND TAKE FOOD FROM MY HAND, BUT SHE WOULD NOT SOAR.

TIME AND AGAIN I WOULD TAKE HER HAWKING, BUT SHE NEVER FLEW HIGHER THAN THE TREETOPS.

ONE DAY MY GREAT-UNCLE SER HARBERT TOLD ME TO TRY A DIFFERENT BIRD. I WAS MAKING A FOOL OF MYSELF WITH PROUDWING, HE SAID, AND HE WAS RIGHT.

"THE SEVEN HAVE NEVER BROUGHT ME SO MUCH AS A SPARROW. IT IS TIME I TRIED ANOTHER HAWK, DAVOS. A RED HAWK."

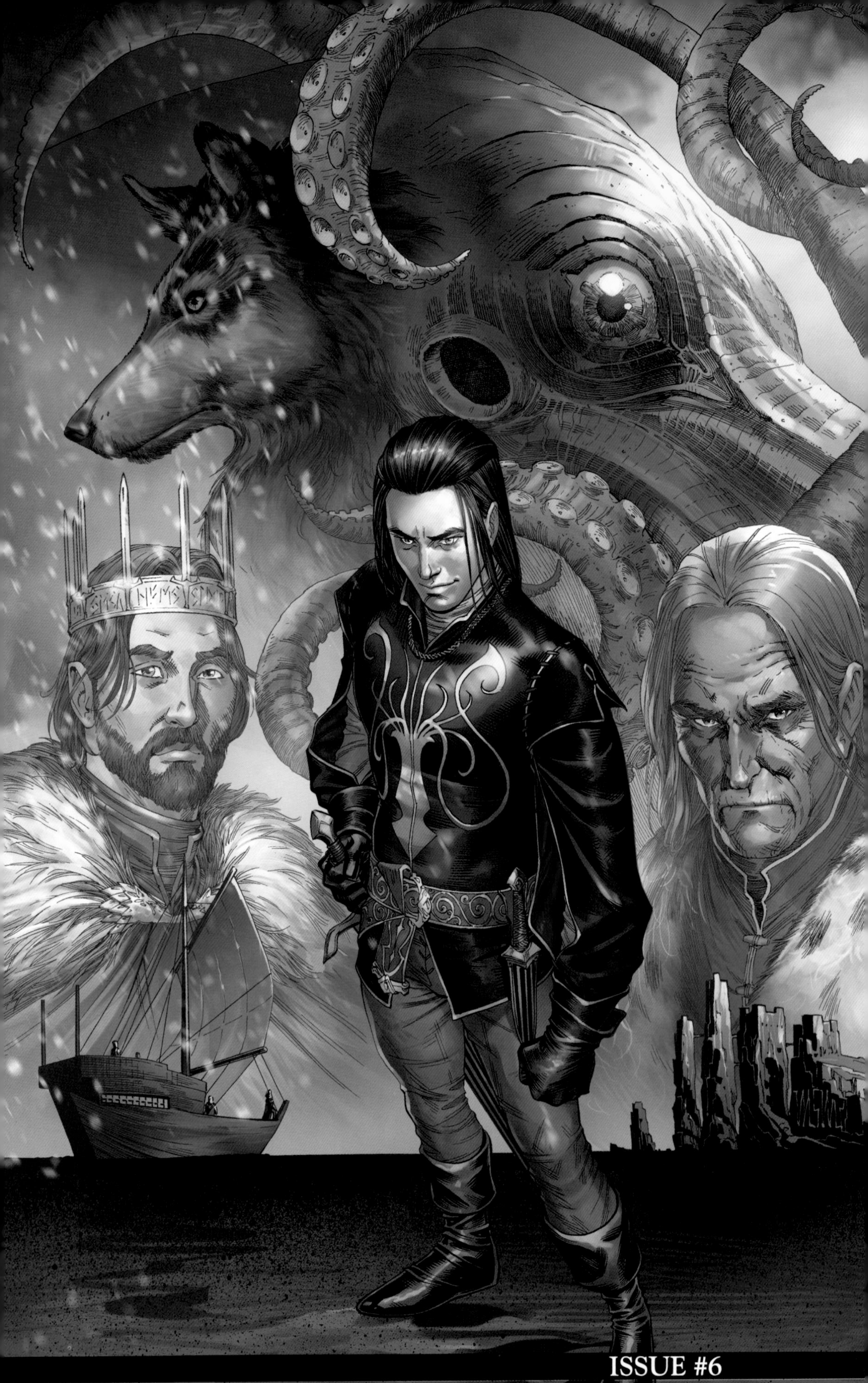

ISSUE #6

ARYA

THE ROAD WAS LITTLE MORE THAN TWO RUTS THROUGH THE WEEDS. THE HUMAN FLOOD THAT HAD FLOWED DOWN THE KINGSROAD WAS ONLY A TRICKLE HERE.

THE GOOD PART WAS, THERE'D BE NO ONE TO POINT THE FINGER AND SAY WHICH WAY THEY'D GONE.

THE BAD PART WAS, THE PATH WAS SO NARROW AND CROOKED THAT THEIR PACE HAD DROPPED TO A CRAWL.

AS FARMLAND GAVE WAY TO FOREST, THE VILLAGES AND HOLDFASTS WERE SMALLER AND FARTHER APART. FOOD GREW HARDER TO COME BY.

IN THE CITY, YOREN HAD LOADED UP THE WAGONS WITH SALT FISH, HARD BREAD, LARD, TURNIPS, SACKS OF BEANS AND BARLEY AND WHEELS OF YELLOW CHEESE, BUT EVERY BITE OF IT HAD BEEN EATEN.

ONE DAY, ARYA CAME ACROSS A FAT RABBIT WITH LONG EARS AND A TWITCHY NOSE. RABBITS RAN FASTER THAN CATS, BUT THEY COULDN'T CLIMB TREES HALF SO WELL.

SHE WHACKED IT WITH HER STICK, AND YOREN STEWED IT WITH SOME MUSHROOMS AND WILD ONIONS.

ARYA WAS GIVEN A WHOLE LEG, SINCE IT WAS HER RABBIT. SHE SHARED IT WITH GENDRY.

THE REST EACH GOT A SPOONFUL, EVEN THE THREE IN MANACLES. JAQEN H'GHAR THANKED HER POLITELY, BUT RORGE ONLY LAUGHED.

THERE'S A HUNTER NOW. LUMPYFACE LUMPYHEAD RABBITKILLER.

AS THE DAYS PASSED, ARYA COULD NOT HELP LOOKING OVER HER SHOULDER, WONDERING WHEN THE GOLD CLOAKS WOULD CATCH THEM.

AT NIGHT, SHE WOKE AT EVERY NOISE TO GRAB FOR NEEDLE'S HILT, AND THEY NEVER MADE CAMP WITHOUT PUTTING OUT SENTRIES.

LOMMY AND THE OTHERS ALL TREATED THE BULL LIKE SOMEONE SPECIAL NOW, BECAUSE THE QUEEN WANTED HIS HEAD, THOUGH HE WOULD HAVE NONE OF IT.

I NEVER DID NOTHING TO NO QUEEN. I DID MY WORK, IS ALL. I WAS S'POSED TO BE AN ARMORER, AND ONE DAY MASTER MOTT SAYS I GOT TO JOIN THE NIGHT'S WATCH.

THAT'S ALL I KNOW.

THEN HE'D GO OFF TO POLISH HIS HELM. IT WAS A BEAUTIFUL HELM, YET HE NEVER ACTUALLY PUT IT ON HIS HEAD.

I BET HE'S THAT TRAITOR'S BASTARD, THE WOLF LORD, THE ONE THEY NICKED ON BAELOR'S STEPS.

HE IS NOT!

HER FATHER ONLY HAD ONE BASTARD, AND THAT WAS JON.

ONE DAY, THEY SPIED A RED GLOW AGAINST THE EVENING SKY.

AS THE WORLD DARKENED, THE FIRE SEEMED TO GROW BRIGHTER AND BRIGHTER, UNTIL IT LOOKED AS THOUGH THE WHOLE NORTH WAS ABLAZE.

IT WAS MIDDAY WHEN THEY ARRIVED AT THE PLACE WHERE THE VILLAGE HAD BEEN.

THE CARCASSES LAY UNDER LIVING BLANKETS OF CARRION CROWS THAT ROSE, CAWING FURIOUSLY, WHEN DISTURBED.

THE TIMBER PALISADE LOOKED STRONG FROM AFAR, BUT HAD NOT PROVED STRONG ENOUGH.

WAIT HERE, AND GUARD THE WAGONS.

A FLOCK OF RAVENS ROSE FROM INSIDE THE WALLS WHEN THEY CLIMBED THROUGH THE BROKEN GATE...

...AND THE CAGED RAVENS IN THEIR WAGONS CALLED OUT TO THEM WITH QUORKS AND RAUCOUS SHRIEKS.

SHOULD WE GO IN AFTER THEM?

YOREN SAID WAIT.

WHEN YOREN FINALLY RETURNED, HE HAD A LITTLE GIRL IN HIS ARMS.

SHE CRIED ALL THE TIME, A WHIMPERY SOUND, LIKE SOMETHING WAS STUCK IN HER THROAT.

EITHER SHE COULDN'T TALK YET OR SHE HAD FORGOTTEN HOW.

MURCH AND CUTJACK WERE CARRYING A WOMAN. HER EYES DIDN'T SEEM TO SEE ANYTHING, EVEN WHEN SHE WAS LOOKING RIGHT AT IT.

PLEASE.

PLEASE. PLEASE.

PLEASE.

LET'S BE QUICK ABOUT IT. COME DARK, THERE'LL BE WOLVES HERE, AND WORSE.

I'M SCARED.

ME TOO.

PLEASE. PLEASE. PLEASE.

ARYA REMEMBERED A STORY OLD NAN HAD TOLD ONCE, ABOUT A MAN IMPRISONED IN A DARK CASTLE BY EVIL GIANTS. HE WAS VERY BRAVE AND SMART AND HE TRICKED THE GIANTS AND ESCAPED...

BUT NO SOONER WAS HE OUTSIDE THE CASTLE THAN THE OTHERS TOOK HIM, AND DRANK HIS HOT RED BLOOD.

NOW SHE KNEW HOW HE MUST HAVE FELT.

THE ONE-ARMED WOMAN DIED AT EVENFALL.

GENDRY AND CUTJACK DUG HER GRAVE ON A HILLSIDE BENEATH A WEEPING WILLOW.

WHEN THE WIND BLEW, ARYA THOUGHT SHE COULD HEAR THE LONG TRAILING BRANCHES WHISPERING...

... "PLEASE. PLEASE. PLEASE."

NO FIRE TONIGHT.

THAT NIGHT, ARYA DRANK TOO MUCH WATER, JUST TO FILL HER BELLY WITH SOMETHING.

WHEN SHE WOKE, HER BLADDER WAS FULL TO BURSTING.

SHE HEARD THE SOFT FOOTFALLS OF A SENTRY, MEN TURNING IN RESTLESS SLEEP...

...AND THE STEADY RHYTHMIC SCRAPE OF STEEL ON STONE.

...QUIET AS A SHADOW...

SHE WAS MAKING WATER, HER CLOTHING TANGLED ABOUT HER ANKLES, WHEN SHE HEARD RUSTLING FROM UNDER THE TREES.

HER BELLY CLENCHED TIGHT AS SHE LACED UP.

ALL SHE COULD THINK WAS HOW STUPID SHE'D BEEN.

TREMBLING, SHE FOLLOWED THE DISTANT SCRAPING SOUND BACK TO CAMP, AND TO YOREN.

WOLVES. IN THE WOODS.

AYE. THEY WOULD BE.

THEY SCARED ME.

DID THEY? SEEMS TO ME YOUR KIND WAS FOND O' WOLVES.

NYMERIA WAS A DIREWOLF. THAT'S DIFFERENT. ANYHOW, SHE'S GONE. JORY AND I THREW ROCKS AT HER UNTIL SHE RAN OFF, OR ELSE THE QUEEN WOULD HAVE KILLED HER.

I BET IF SHE'D BEEN IN THE CITY, SHE WOULDN'T HAVE LET THEM CUT OFF FATHER'S HEAD.

ORPHAN BOYS GOT NO FATHERS, OR DID YOU FORGET THAT?

THE ONLY WOLVES WE GOT TO FEAR ARE THE ONES WEAR MANSKIN, LIKE THOSE WHO DONE FOR THAT VILLAGE.

I WISH I WAS HOME.

MIGHT BE I SHOULD OF LEFT YOU WHERE I FOUND YOU, BOY. ALL OF YOU. SAFER IN THE CITY, SEEMS TO ME.

BEEN BRINGING MEN TO THE WALL FOR CLOSE ON THIRTY YEARS. ALL THAT TIME, I ONLY LOST THREE. OLD MAN DIED OF A FEVER, CITY BOY GOT SNAKEBIT TAKING A SHIT, AND ONE FOOL TRIED TO KILL ME IN MY SLEEP AND GOT A RED SMILE FOR HIS TROUBLE.

THREE IN THIRTY YEARS. GO TO SLEEP, BOY. HEAR ME?

SHE DID TRY. YET AS SHE LAY UNDER HER THIN BLANKET, SHE COULD HEAR WOLVES HOWLING...

...AND ANOTHER SOUND, FAINTER, NO MORE THAN A WHISPER ON THE WIND, THAT MIGHT HAVE BEEN SCREAMS.

THEON

THERE WAS NO SAFE ANCHORAGE AT PYKE, BUT THEON GREYJOY WISHED TO LOOK UPON HIS FATHER'S CASTLE FROM THE SEA, AS HE HAD SEEN IT TEN YEARS BEFORE, WHEN ROBERT BARATHEON'S WAR GALLEY HAD BORNE HIM AWAY TO BE A WARD OF EDDARD STARK.

THE POINT OF LAND ON WHICH THE GREYJOYS HAD RAISED THEIR FORTRESS HAD THRUST LIKE A SWORD INTO THE BOWELS OF THE OCEAN, BUT THE WAVES HAD HAMMERED AT IT DAY AND NIGHT UNTIL THE LAND BROKE AND SHATTERED, THOUSANDS OF YEARS PAST.

THEON HAD NEVER SEEN A MORE STIRRING SIGHT.

DOES THE CASTLE LOOK AS YOU REMEMBER IT, MILORD?

IT LOOKS SMALLER—THOUGH PERHAPS THAT IS ONLY THE DISTANCE.

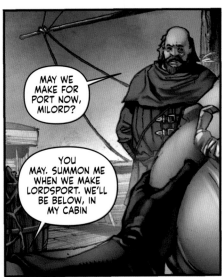

MAY WE MAKE FOR PORT NOW, MILORD?

YOU MAY. SUMMON ME WHEN WE MAKE LORDSPORT. WE'LL BE BELOW, IN MY CABIN

THE CABIN WAS THE CAPTAIN'S, IN TRUTH, BUT IT HAD BEEN TURNED OVER TO THEON'S USE.

THE CAPTAIN'S DAUGHTER HAD NOT BEEN, BUT SHE HAD COME TO HIS BED WILLINGLY ENOUGH ALL THE SAME.

SHE HAD BEEN A MAIDEN THE FIRST TIME HE TOOK HER. THAT WAS SURPRISING AT HER AGE, BUT THEON FOUND IT DIVERTING.

TAKE OFF YOUR CLOAK.

HE DID NOT THINK THE CAPTAIN APPROVED, AND THAT WAS AMUSING AS WELL, WATCHING THE MAN STRUGGLE TO SWALLOW HIS OUTRAGE, THE RICH PURSE OF GOLD HE'D BEEN PROMISED NEVER FAR FROM HIS THOUGHTS.

I COULD GO ASHORE WITH YOU. I WOULD, IF IT PLEASE YOU...

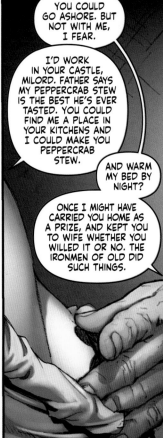

YOU COULD GO ASHORE. BUT NOT WITH ME, I FEAR.

I'D WORK IN YOUR CASTLE, MILORD. FATHER SAYS MY PEPPERCRAB STEW IS THE BEST HE'S EVER TASTED. YOU COULD FIND ME A PLACE IN YOUR KITCHENS AND I COULD MAKE YOU PEPPERCRAB STEW.

AND WARM MY BED BY NIGHT?

ONCE I MIGHT HAVE CARRIED YOU HOME AS A PRIZE, AND KEPT YOU TO WIFE WHETHER YOU WILLED IT OR NO. THE IRONMEN OF OLD DID SUCH THINGS.

A MAN HAD HIS ROCK WIFE, HIS TRUE BRIDE, IRONBORN LIKE HIMSELF, BUT HE HAD HIS SALT WIVES TOO, WOMEN CAPTURED ON RAIDS.

I WOULD BE YOUR SALT WIFE, MILORD.

I FEAR THOSE DAYS ARE GONE. NOW...

...UNLACE ME AND PLEASURE ME WITH YOUR MOUTH.

WE'RE OUT OF OLDTOWN, BEARING APPLES AND ORANGES, WINES FROM THE ARBOR, FEATHERS FROM THE SUMMER ISLES.

AND I'VE BROUGHT YOUR HEIR BACK TO YOU.

HE SAW NO FAMILIAR FACES, NO HONOR GUARD WAITING TO ESCORT HIM FROM LORDSPORT TO PYKE.

YET A GREAT NUMBER OF LONGSHIPS, FIFTY OR SIXTY AT THE LEAST, STOOD OUT TO SEA OR LAY BEACHED. HAD LORD BALON CALLED THE GREYJOY BANNERS?

I REQUIRE A HORSE...

THAT WILL NOT BE NEEDED.

NEPHEW THEON. YOUR LORD FATHER BID ME FETCH YOU. COME.

UNCLE AERON?

IN ONE OF HIS RARE CURT LETTERS, LORD BALON HAD WRITTEN OF HIS YOUNGEST BROTHER GOING DOWN IN A STORM, AND TURNING HOLY WHEN HE WASHED UP SAFE ON SHORE.

I HAD NOT LOOKED FOR YOU, UNCLE. AFTER TEN YEARS, I THOUGHT PERHAPS MY LORD FATHER AND LADY MOTHER MIGHT COME THEMSELVES, OR SEND DAGMER WITH AN HONOR GUARD.

TELL ME TRUE, NEPHEW. DO YOU PRAY TO THE WOLF GODS NOW?

NED STARK PRAYED TO A TREE. NO, I CARE NOTHING FOR STARK'S GODS.

GOOD. KNEEL.

UNCLE, I—

KNEEL. OR ARE YOU TOO PROUD NOW, A LORDLING OF THE GREEN LANDS COME AMONG US?

THEON HAD A PURPOSE HERE AND MIGHT NEED AERON'S HELP TO ACHIEVE IT. A CROWN WAS WORTH A LITTLE MUD AND HORSESHIT ON HIS BREECHES.

BOW YOUR HEAD.

LET THEON YOUR SERVANT BE BORN AGAIN FROM THE SEA, AS YOU WERE. BLESS HIM WITH SALT, BLESS HIM WITH STONE, BLESS HIM WITH STEEL. NEPHEW, DO YOU STILL KNOW THE WORDS?

WHAT IS DEAD MAY NEVER DIE...

...BUT RISES AGAIN, HARDER AND STRONGER.

STAND.

I HAVE BEEN HALF MY LIFE AWAY FROM HOME. WILL I FIND THE ISLANDS CHANGED?

MEN FISH THE SEA, DIG IN THE EARTH, AND DIE. WOMEN BIRTH CHILDREN IN BLOOD AND PAIN, AND DIE. NIGHT FOLLOWS DAY. THE WINDS AND TIDES REMAIN. THE ISLANDS ARE AS OUR GOD MADE THEM.

WILL I FIND MY SISTER AND MY LADY MOTHER AT PYKE?

YOU WILL NOT. YOUR MOTHER DWELLS ON HARLAW, WITH HER OWN SISTER. IT IS LESS RAW THERE, AND HER COUGH TROUBLES HER. YOUR SISTER ASHA HAS TAKEN *BLACK WIND* TO GREAT WYK, WITH MESSAGES FROM YOUR LORD FATHER. SHE WILL RETURN E'ER LONG.

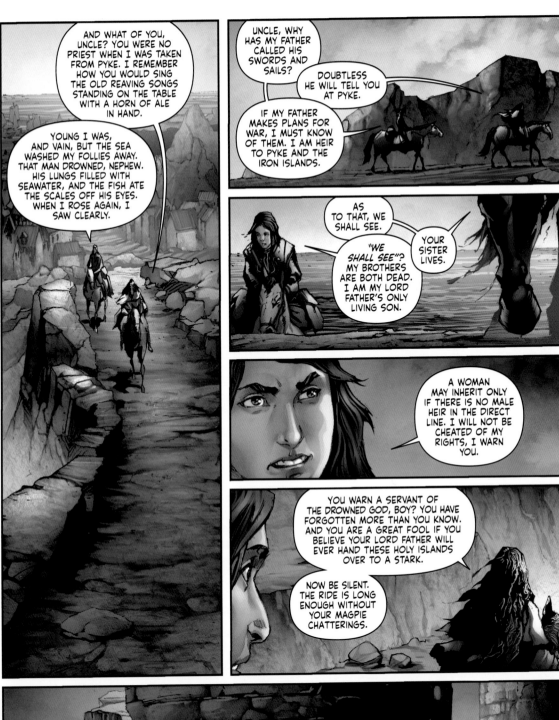

AND WHAT OF YOU, UNCLE? YOU WERE NO PRIEST WHEN I WAS TAKEN FROM PYKE. I REMEMBER HOW YOU WOULD SING THE OLD REAVING SONGS STANDING ON THE TABLE WITH A HORN OF ALE IN HAND.

YOUNG I WAS, AND VAIN, BUT THE SEA WASHED MY FOLLIES AWAY. THAT MAN DROWNED, NEPHEW. HIS LUNGS FILLED WITH SEAWATER, AND THE FISH ATE THE SCALES OFF HIS EYES. WHEN I ROSE AGAIN, I SAW CLEARLY.

UNCLE, WHY HAS MY FATHER CALLED HIS SWORDS AND SAILS?

DOUBTLESS HE WILL TELL YOU AT PYKE.

IF MY FATHER MAKES PLANS FOR WAR, I MUST KNOW OF THEM. I AM HEIR TO PYKE AND THE IRON ISLANDS.

AS TO THAT, WE SHALL SEE.

YOUR SISTER LIVES.

"WE SHALL SEE"? MY BROTHERS ARE BOTH DEAD. I AM MY LORD FATHER'S ONLY LIVING SON.

A WOMAN MAY INHERIT ONLY IF THERE IS NO MALE HEIR IN THE DIRECT LINE. I WILL NOT BE CHEATED OF MY RIGHTS, I WARN YOU.

YOU WARN A SERVANT OF THE DROWNED GOD, BOY? YOU HAVE FORGOTTEN MORE THAN YOU KNOW. AND YOU ARE A GREAT FOOL IF YOU BELIEVE YOUR LORD FATHER WILL EVER HAND THESE HOLY ISLANDS OVER TO A STARK.

NOW BE SILENT. THE RIDE IS LONG ENOUGH WITHOUT YOUR MAGPIE CHATTERINGS.

TO GET TO THE SEA TOWER ON ITS CROOKED PILLAR, THEON HAD TO CROSS THREE BRIDGES, EACH NARROWER THAN THE ONE BEFORE.

THE LAST WAS MADE OF ROPE AND WOOD, AND THE WET SALT WIND MADE IT SWAY UNDERFOOT LIKE A LIVING THING. THEON'S HEART WAS IN HIS MOUTH BY THE TIME HE WAS HALFWAY ACROSS.

AS A BOY, HE USED TO RUN ACROSS THIS BRIDGE, EVEN IN THE BLACK OF NIGHT. BOYS BELIEVE NOTHING CAN HURT THEM, HIS DOUBT WHISPERED. GROWN MEN KNOW BETTER.

BALON GREYJOY HAD ALWAYS BEEN THIN, BUT NOW HE LOOKED AS THOUGH THE GODS HAD PUT HIM IN A CAULDRON AND BOILED EVERY SPARE OUNCE OF FLESH FROM HIS BONES, UNTIL NOTHING REMAINED BUT HAIR AND SKIN.

NINE YEARS, IS IT?

TEN.

A BOY THEY TOOK. WHAT ARE YOU NOW?

A MAN. YOUR BLOOD AND YOUR HEIR.

WE SHALL SEE.

YOU SHALL.

I BRING A LETTER—

DID NED STARK DRESS YOU LIKE THAT?

WAS IT HIS PLEASURE TO GARB YOU IN VELVETS AND SILKS AND MAKE YOU HIS OWN SWEET DAUGHTER?

THAT BAUBLE AROUND YOUR NECK—WAS IT BOUGHT WITH GOLD OR IRON?

IT HAD BEEN SO LONG, HE HAD FORGOTTEN.

IN THE OLD WAY, WOMEN MIGHT DECORATE THEMSELVES WITH ORNAMENTS BOUGHT WITH COIN, BUT A WARRIOR WORE ONLY THE JEWELRY HE TOOK OFF THE CORPSES OF ENEMIES SLAIN WITH HIS OWN HAND.

"PAYING THE IRON PRICE," IT WAS CALLED.

YOU BLUSH RED AS A MAID, THEON. A QUESTION WAS ASKED. IS IT THE GOLD PRICE YOU PAID, OR THE IRON?

THE GOLD.

MY DAUGHTER HAS TAKEN AN AXE FOR A LOVER. I WILL NOT HAVE MY SON BEDECK HIMSELF LIKE A WHORE.

IT IS AS I FEARED. THE GREEN LANDS HAVE MADE YOU SOFT, AND THE STARKS HAVE MADE YOU THEIRS.

YOU'RE WRONG. NED STARK WAS MY GAOLER, BUT MY BLOOD IS STILL SALT AND IRON.

YET THE STARK PUP SENDS YOU TO ME LIKE A WELL-TRAINED RAVEN, CLUTCHING HIS LITTLE MESSAGE.

THERE IS NOTHING SMALL ABOUT THE LETTER I BEAR. AND THE OFFER HE MAKES IS ONE *I* SUGGESTED TO HIM.

THIS WOLF KING HEEDS YOUR COUNSEL, DOES HE?

HE HEEDS ME, YES. I'VE HUNTED WITH HIM, TRAINED WITH HIM, SHARED MEAT AND MEAD WITH HIM, WARRED AT HIS SIDE. I HAVE EARNED HIS TRUST. HE LOOKS ON ME AS AN OLDER BROTHER—

NO. NOT HERE, NOT IN PYKE, NOT IN MY HEARING. YOU WILL NOT NAME HIM *BROTHER*, THIS SON OF THE MAN WHO PUT YOUR TRUE BROTHERS TO THE SWORD.

OR HAVE YOU FORGOTTEN RODRIK AND MARON, WHO WERE YOUR OWN BLOOD?

I FORGET NOTHING.

NED STARK HAD KILLED NEITHER OF HIS BROTHERS, IN TRUTH. RODRIK HAD BEEN SLAIN BY LORD JASON MALLISTER AT SEAGARD, MARON CRUSHED IN THE COLLAPSE OF THE OLD SOUTH TOWER...BUT STARK WOULD HAVE DONE FOR THEM JUST AS QUICK HAD THE TIDE OF BATTLE SWEPT THEM TOGETHER.

I REMEMBER MY BROTHERS VERY WELL.

CHIEFLY, HE REMEMBERED RODRIK'S DRUNKEN CUFFS AND MARON'S CRUEL JAPES AND ENDLESS LIES.

I REMEMBER WHEN MY FATHER WAS A KING TOO.

HERE. READ IT...YOUR GRACE.

SO...

...THE BOY WOULD GIVE ME A CROWN AGAIN. AND ALL I NEED DO IS DESTROY HIS ENEMIES.

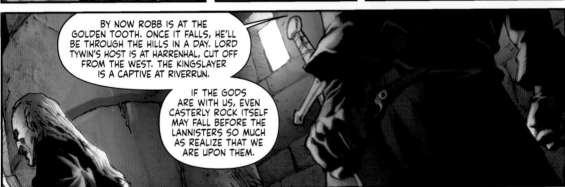

BY NOW ROBB IS AT THE GOLDEN TOOTH. ONCE IT FALLS, HE'LL BE THROUGH THE HILLS IN A DAY. LORD TYWIN'S HOST IS AT HARRENHAL, CUT OFF FROM THE WEST. THE KINGSLAYER IS A CAPTIVE AT RIVERRUN.

IF THE GODS ARE WITH US, EVEN CASTERLY ROCK ITSELF MAY FALL BEFORE THE LANNISTERS SO MUCH AS REALIZE THAT WE ARE UPON THEM.

CASTERLY ROCK HAS NEVER FALLEN.

UNTIL NOW.

SO THIS IS WHY ROBB STARK SENDS YOU BACK TO ME, AFTER SO LONG? SO YOU MIGHT WIN MY CONSENT TO THIS PLAN OF HIS?

IT IS MY PLAN, NOT ROBB'S.

HIS, AS THE VICTORY WOULD BE, AND IN TIME THE CROWN.

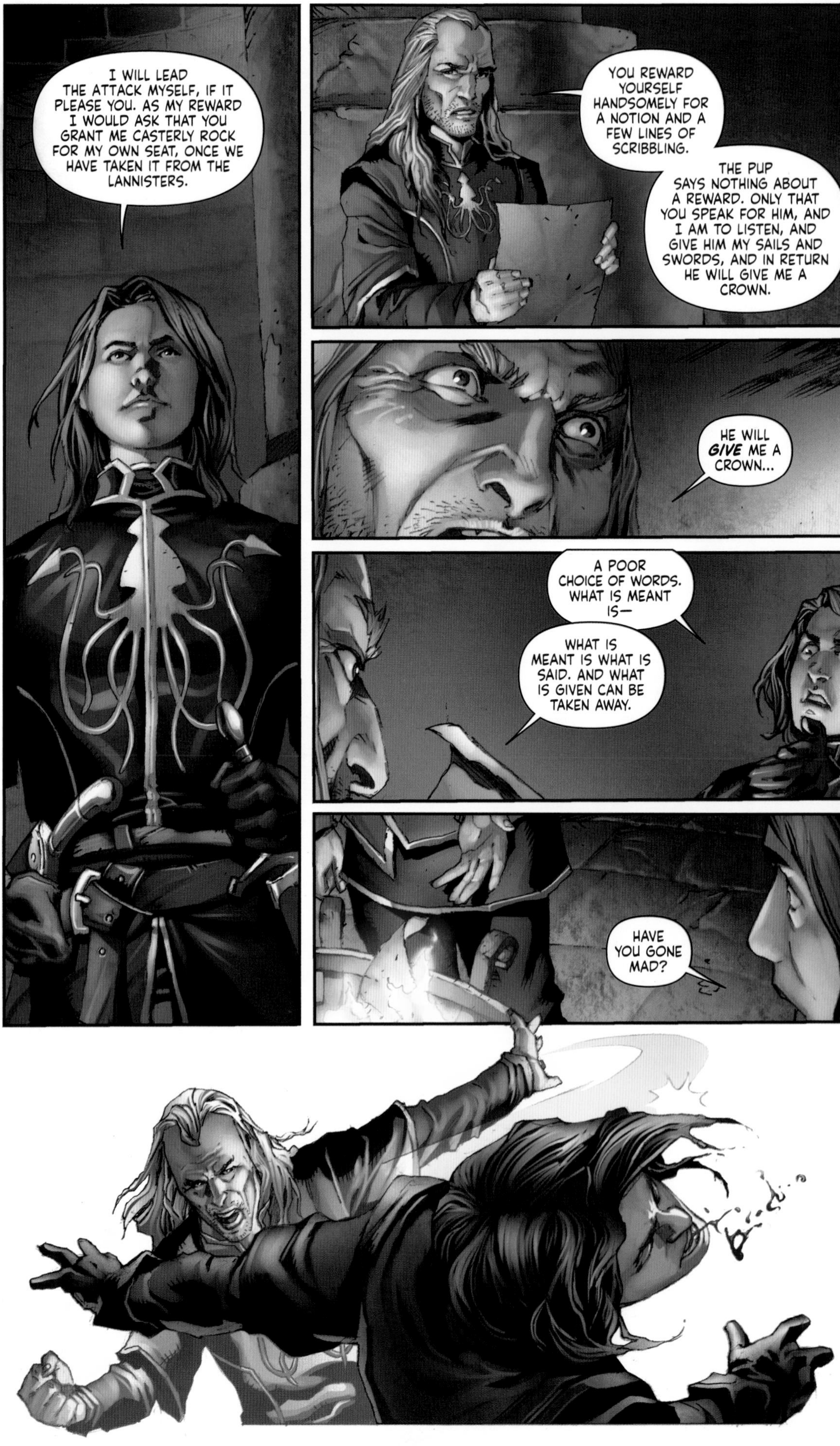
I WILL LEAD THE ATTACK MYSELF, IF IT PLEASE YOU. AS MY REWARD I WOULD ASK THAT YOU GRANT ME CASTERLY ROCK FOR MY OWN SEAT, ONCE WE HAVE TAKEN IT FROM THE LANNISTERS.
YOU REWARD YOURSELF HANDSOMELY FOR A NOTION AND A FEW LINES OF SCRIBBLING.
THE PUP SAYS NOTHING ABOUT A REWARD. ONLY THAT YOU SPEAK FOR HIM, AND I AM TO LISTEN, AND GIVE HIM MY SAILS AND SWORDS, AND IN RETURN HE WILL GIVE ME A CROWN.
HE WILL ***GIVE*** ME A CROWN...
A POOR CHOICE OF WORDS. WHAT IS MEANT IS—
WHAT IS MEANT IS WHAT IS SAID. AND WHAT IS GIVEN CAN BE TAKEN AWAY.
HAVE YOU GONE MAD?

MIND YOUR TONGUE. YOU ARE NOT IN WINTERFELL NOW, AND I AM NOT ROBB THE BOY, THAT YOU SHOULD SPEAK TO ME SO.

I AM THE GREYJOY, LORD REAPER OF PYKE, KING OF SALT AND ROCK, SON OF THE SEA WIND, AND NO MAN *GIVES* ME A CROWN.

I PAY THE IRON PRICE. I WILL *TAKE* MY CROWN, AS URRON REDHAND DID FIVE THOUSAND YEARS AGO.

TAKE IT, THEN. CALL YOURSELF KING OF THE IRON ISLANDS, NO ONE WILL CARE...

...UNTIL THE WARS ARE OVER, AND THE VICTOR LOOKS ABOUT AND SPIES THE OLD FOOL PERCHED OFF HIS SHORE WITH AN IRON CROWN ON HIS HEAD!

WELL, AT THE LEAST YOU ARE NO CRAVEN. NO MORE THAN I'M A FOOL.

DO YOU THINK I GATHER MY SHIPS TO WATCH THEM ROCK AT ANCHOR? I MEAN TO CARVE OUT A KINGDOM WITH FIRE AND SWORD...BUT NOT FROM THE WEST, AND NOT AT THE BIDDING OF KING ROBB THE BOY.

CASTERLY ROCK IS TOO STRONG, AND LORD TYWIN TOO CUNNING BY HALF. AYE, WE MIGHT TAKE LANNISPORT, BUT WE SHOULD NEVER KEEP IT.

NO. I HUNGER FOR A DIFFERENT PLUM...NOT SO JUICY SWEET, TO BE SURE, YET IT HANGS THERE RIPE AND UNDEFENDED.

WHERE? THEON MIGHT HAVE ASKED, BUT BY THEN HE KNEW.

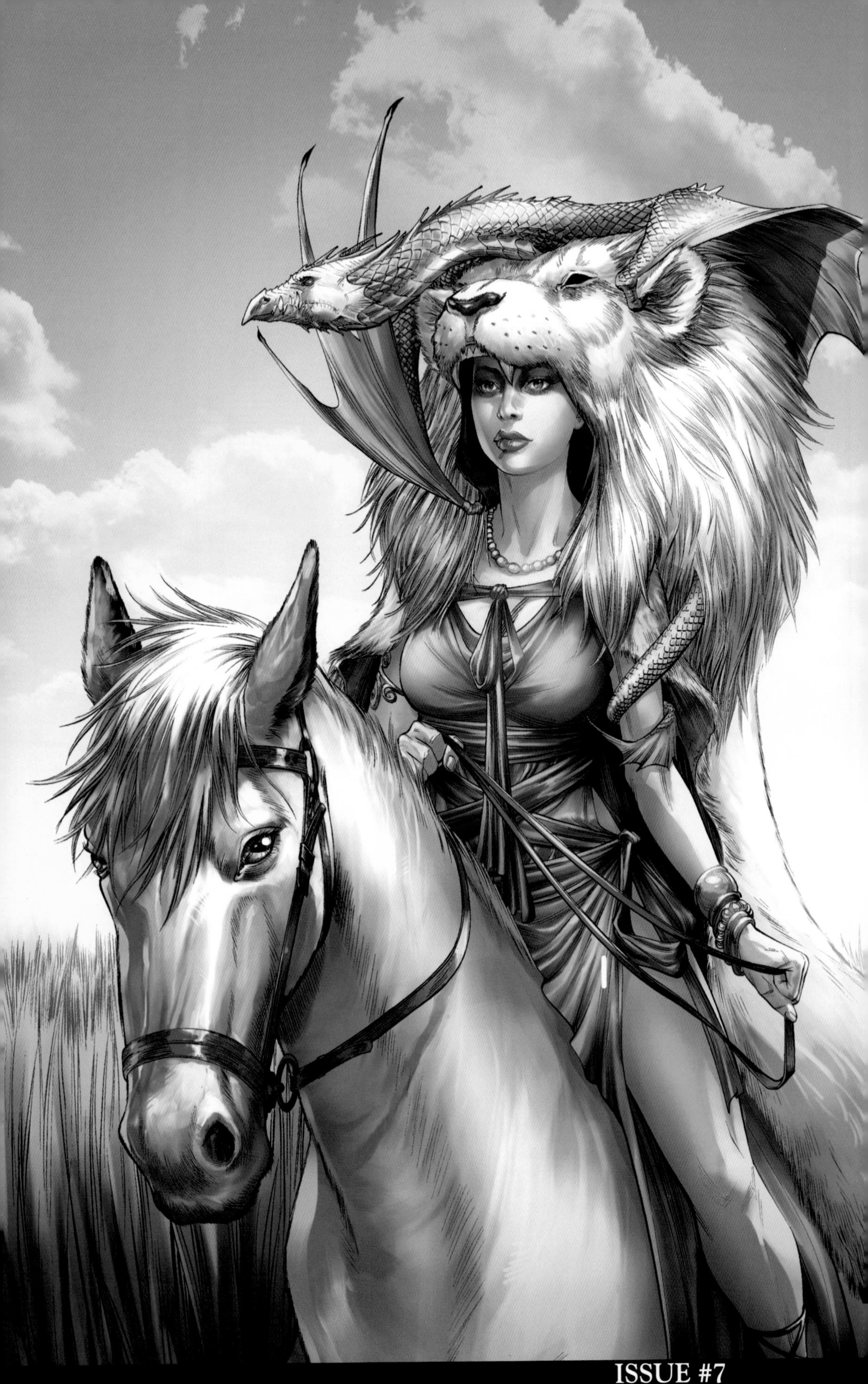

ISSUE #7

JON

WHITETREE, THE VILLAGE WAS NAMED ON SAM'S OLD MAPS.

ABOVE IT LOOMED THE BIGGEST WEIRWOOD JON SNOW HAD EVER SEEN.

THE SIZE DID NOT DISTURB HIM SO MUCH AS THE FACE...THE MOUTH ESPECIALLY, NO SIMPLE CARVED SLASH, BUT A JAGGED HOLLOW LARGE ENOUGH TO SWALLOW A SHEEP.

THOSE WERE NOT SHEEP BONES, THOUGH. NOR WAS THAT A SHEEP'S SKULL IN THE ASHES.

AN OLD TREE.

OLD. OLD, OLD, OLD.

AND POWERFUL, JON THOUGHT.

LOOK AT THAT FACE. SMALL WONDER MEN FEARED THEM, WHEN THEY FIRST CAME TO WESTEROS. I'D LIKE TO TAKE AN AXE TO THE BLOODY THING MYSELF.

MY LORD FATHER BELIEVED NO MAN COULD TELL A LIE IN FRONT OF A HEART TREE. THE OLD GODS KNOW WHEN MEN ARE LYING.

MY FATHER BELIEVED THE SAME. LET ME HAVE A LOOK AT THAT SKULL.

THE WILDLINGS BURN THEIR DEAD. WE'VE ALWAYS KNOWN THAT. NOW I WISHED I'D ASKED THEM WHY, WHEN THERE WERE STILL A FEW AROUND TO ASK.

JON REMEMBERED THE WIGHT RISING, ITS EYES SHINING BLUE IN THE PALE DEAD FACE. HE KNEW WHY, HE WAS CERTAIN.

WOULD THAT BONES COULD TALK. THIS FELLOW COULD TELL US MUCH.

HOW HE DIED. WHO BURNED HIM, AND WHY. WHERE THE WILDLINGS HAVE GONE.

GO THROUGH ALL THESE HOUSES. GIANT, GO TO THE TOP OF THIS TREE AND HAVE A LOOK.

PERCHANCE THIS TIME THE TRAIL WILL BE FRESHER.

JON WAS PAIRED WITH DOUR EDDISON TOLLETT, WHOM THE OTHERS CALLED DOLOROUS EDD.

BAD ENOUGH WHEN THE DEAD COME WALKING. NOW THE OLD BEAR WANTS THEM TALKING AS WELL?

NO GOOD WILL COME OF THAT, I WARRANT. THE DEAD ARE LIKELY DULL FELLOWS, FULL OF TEDIOUS COMPLAINTS— THE GROUND'S TOO COLD, MY GRAVESTONE SHOULD BE LARGER, WHY DOES *HE* GET MORE WORMS THAN I DO...

WHAT A DISMAL PLACE TO LIVE.

I WAS BORN IN A HOUSE MUCH LIKE THIS. THOSE WERE MY ENCHANTED YEARS. LATER I FELL ON HARD TIMES.

THERE'S NOTHING HERE.

NOTHING WAS WHAT HE HAD EXPECTED.

WHAT DO YOU THINK HAPPENED TO THEM ALL?

SOMETHING WORSE THAN WE CAN IMAGINE.

WHITETREE WAS THE FOURTH VILLAGE THEY HAD PASSED, AND IT HAD BEEN THE SAME IN ALL OF THEM. THE PEOPLE WERE GONE, VANISHED WITH THEIR SCANT POSSESSIONS AND WHATEVER ANIMALS THEY MAY HAVE HAD.

NONE OF THE VILLAGES SHOWED ANY SIGNS OF HAVING BEEN ATTACKED. THEY WERE SIMPLY...EMPTY.

WELL, *I* MIGHT BE ABLE TO IMAGINE IT, BUT I'D SOONER NOT. BAD ENOUGH TO KNOW YOU'RE GOING TO COME TO SOME AWFUL END WITHOUT THINKING ABOUT IT AFORETIME.

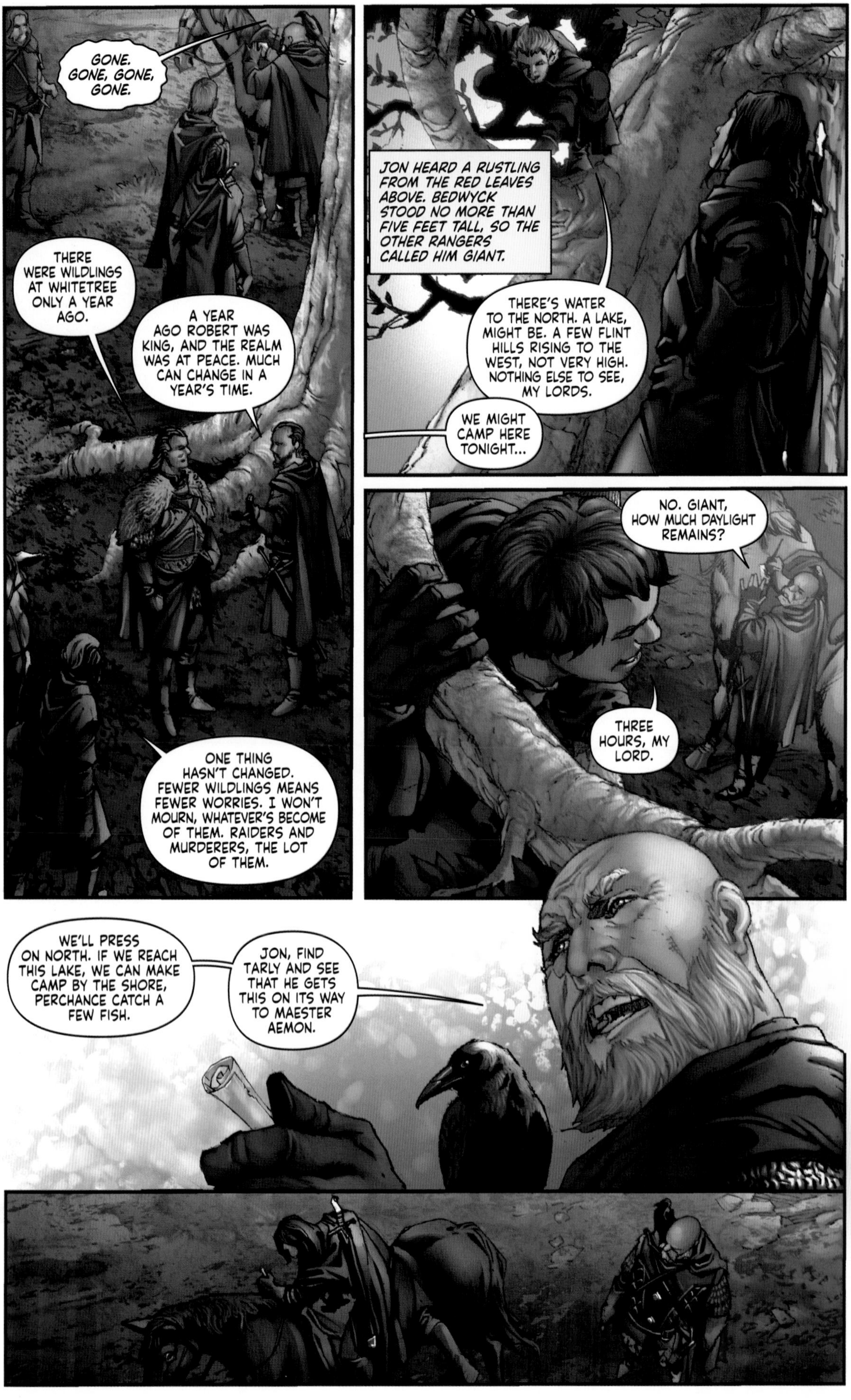
GONE. GONE, GONE, GONE.
THERE WERE WILDLINGS AT WHITETREE ONLY A YEAR AGO.
A YEAR AGO ROBERT WAS KING, AND THE REALM WAS AT PEACE. MUCH CAN CHANGE IN A YEAR'S TIME.
ONE THING HASN'T CHANGED. FEWER WILDLINGS MEANS FEWER WORRIES. I WON'T MOURN, WHATEVER'S BECOME OF THEM. RAIDERS AND MURDERERS, THE LOT OF THEM.
JON HEARD A RUSTLING FROM THE RED LEAVES ABOVE. BEDWYCK STOOD NO MORE THAN FIVE FEET TALL, SO THE OTHER RANGERS CALLED HIM GIANT.
THERE'S WATER TO THE NORTH. A LAKE, MIGHT BE. A FEW FLINT HILLS RISING TO THE WEST, NOT VERY HIGH. NOTHING ELSE TO SEE, MY LORDS.
WE MIGHT CAMP HERE TONIGHT...
NO. GIANT, HOW MUCH DAYLIGHT REMAINS?
THREE HOURS, MY LORD.
WE'LL PRESS ON NORTH. IF WE REACH THIS LAKE, WE CAN MAKE CAMP BY THE SHORE, PERCHANCE CATCH A FEW FISH.
JON, FIND TARLY AND SEE THAT HE GETS THIS ON ITS WAY TO MAESTER AEMON.

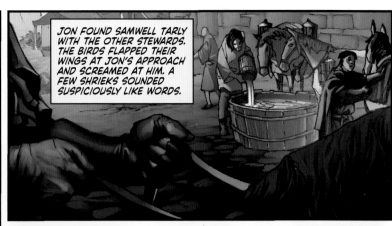

JON FOUND SAMWELL TARLY WITH THE OTHER STEWARDS. THE BIRDS FLAPPED THEIR WINGS AT JON'S APPROACH AND SCREAMED AT HIM. A FEW SHRIEKS SOUNDED SUSPICIOUSLY LIKE WORDS.

CAW

HAVE YOU BEEN TEACHING THEM TO TALK?

CAW CAW CAW!

A FEW WORDS. THREE OF THEM CAN SAY *SNOW.*

WAS THERE ANYTHING IN WHITETREE?

BONES, ASHES, AND EMPTY HOUSES.

THE OLD BEAR WANTS WORD SENT BACK TO AEMON.

FLY HOME NOW, BRAVE ONE. HOME.

I WISH HE COULD CARRY ME WITH HIM.

STILL?

YES, BUT...I'M NOT AS FRIGHTENED AS I WAS, TRULY. THE FIRST NIGHT, EVERY TIME I HEARD SOMEONE GETTING UP TO MAKE WATER, I THOUGHT IT WAS WILDLINGS CREEPING IN TO SLIT MY THROAT.

I WAS AFRAID THAT IF I CLOSED MY EYES, I MIGHT NEVER OPEN THEM AGAIN. ONLY...DAWN CAME AFTER ALL.

I MAY BE CRAVEN, BUT I'M NOT STUPID. I'M SORE AND MY BACK ACHES FROM RIDING AND FROM SLEEPING ON THE GROUND, BUT I'M HARDLY SCARED AT ALL.

THE WORLD IS STRANGE, JON THOUGHT...

...TWO HUNDRED BRAVE MEN HAD LEFT THE WALL, AND THE ONLY ONE WHO WAS **NOT** GROWING MORE FEARFUL WAS SAM, THE SELF-CONFESSED COWARD.

WE'LL MAKE A RANGER OF YOU YET. NEXT THING, YOU'LL WANT TO BE AN OUTRIDER LIKE GRENN. SHALL I SPEAK TO THE OLD BEAR?

DON'T YOU DARE!

I HAD HOPED WE MIGHT STAY THE NIGHT IN THE VILLAGE. IT WOULD BE NICE TO SLEEP UNDER A ROOF AGAIN.

TOO FEW ROOFS FOR ALL OF US.

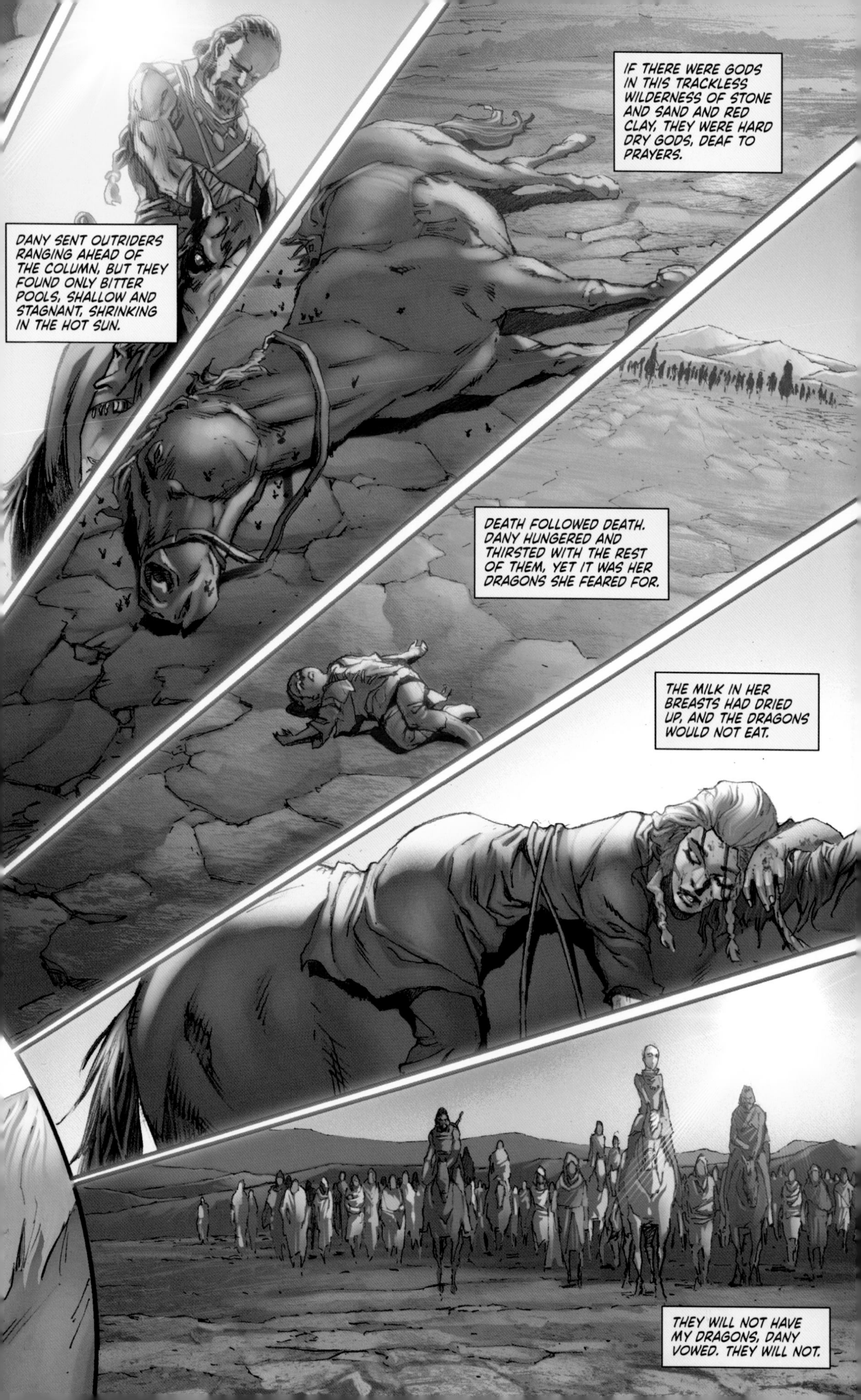
DANY SENT OUTRIDERS RANGING AHEAD OF THE COLUMN, BUT THEY FOUND ONLY BITTER POOLS, SHALLOW AND STAGNANT, SHRINKING IN THE HOT SUN.
IF THERE WERE GODS IN THIS TRACKLESS WILDERNESS OF STONE AND SAND AND RED CLAY, THEY WERE HARD DRY GODS, DEAF TO PRAYERS.
DEATH FOLLOWED DEATH. DANY HUNGERED AND THIRSTED WITH THE REST OF THEM, YET IT WAS HER DRAGONS SHE FEARED FOR.
THE MILK IN HER BREASTS HAD DRIED UP, AND THE DRAGONS WOULD NOT EAT.
THEY WILL NOT HAVE MY DRAGONS, DANY VOWED. THEY WILL NOT.

THE DRAGONS WOULD HISS AND SPIT AT EACH BLOODY MORSEL OF HORSEMEAT, STEAM RISING FROM THEIR NOSTRILS, YET THEY WOULD NOT TAKE THE FOOD...UNTIL DANY REMEMBERED SOMETHING VISERYS HAD TOLD HER.

ONLY DRAGONS AND MEN EAT COOKED MEAT.

AEGON'S DRAGONS WERE NAMED FOR THE GODS OF OLD VALYRIA.

VISENYA'S DRAGON WAS VHAGAR, RHAENYS HAD MERAXES, AND AEGON RODE BALERION, THE BLACK DREAD.

IT WAS SAID THAT BALERION'S FIRE WAS AS BLACK AS HIS SCALES, AND HIS WINGS SO VAST THAT WHOLE TOWNS WERE SWALLOWED UP IN THEIR SHADOW WHEN HE PASSED OVERHEAD.

KHALEESI, THERE SITS BALERION, COME AGAIN.

IT MAY BE AS YOU SAY, BLOOD OF MY BLOOD, BUT HE SHALL HAVE A NEW NAME FOR THIS NEW LIFE. I WOULD NAME THEM ALL FOR THOSE THE GODS HAVE TAKEN.

THE GREEN ONE SHALL BE RHAEGAL, FOR MY VALIANT BROTHER WHO DIED ON THE GREEN BANKS OF THE TRIDENT.

THE CREAM-AND-GOLD I CALL VISERION. VISERYS WAS CRUEL AND WEAK AND FRIGHTENED, YET HE WAS MY BROTHER STILL. HIS DRAGON WILL DO WHAT HE COULD NOT.

AND THE BLACK BEAST?

THE BLACK...IS DROGON.

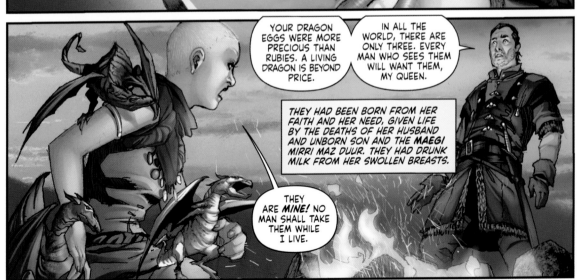

YOUR DRAGON EGGS WERE MORE PRECIOUS THAN RUBIES. A LIVING DRAGON IS BEYOND PRICE.

IN ALL THE WORLD, THERE ARE ONLY THREE. EVERY MAN WHO SEES THEM WILL WANT THEM, MY QUEEN.

THEY HAD BEEN BORN FROM HER FAITH AND HER NEED, GIVEN LIFE BY THE DEATHS OF HER HUSBAND AND UNBORN SON AND THE MAEGI MIRRI MAZ DUUR. THEY HAD DRUNK MILK FROM HER SWOLLEN BREASTS.

THEY ARE MINE! NO MAN SHALL TAKE THEM WHILE I LIVE.

YET EVEN AS HER DRAGONS PROSPERED, HER KHALASAR WITHERED AND DIED. AROUND THEM THE LAND TURNED EVER MORE DESOLATE.

HORSES DROPPED IN THEIR TRACKS, LEAVING SO FEW THAT SOME OF HER PEOPLE MUST TRUDGE ALONG ON FOOT.

DOREAH TOOK A FEVER AND GREW WORSE WITH EVERY LEAGUE THEY CROSSED. HER LIPS AND HANDS BROKE WITH BLOOD BLISTERS, AND HER HAIR CAME OUT IN CLUMPS.

ONE EVENFALL SHE LACKED THE STRENGTH TO MOUNT HER HORSE.

JHOGO SAID THEY MUST LEAVE HER, BUT DANY REMEMBERED A NIGHT ON THE DOTHRAKI SEA, WHEN THE LYSENE GIRL HAD TAUGHT HER SECRETS SO THAT DROGO MIGHT LOVE HER MORE.

SHE GAVE DOREAH WATER FROM HER OWN SKIN, AND HELD HER HAND UNTIL SHE DIED. ONLY THEN WOULD SHE PERMIT THE KHALASAR TO PRESS ON.

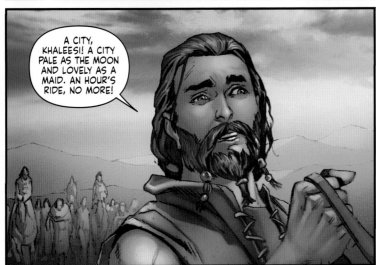

A CITY, KHALEESI! A CITY PALE AS THE MOON AND LOVELY AS A MAID. AN HOUR'S RIDE, NO MORE!

SHOW ME.

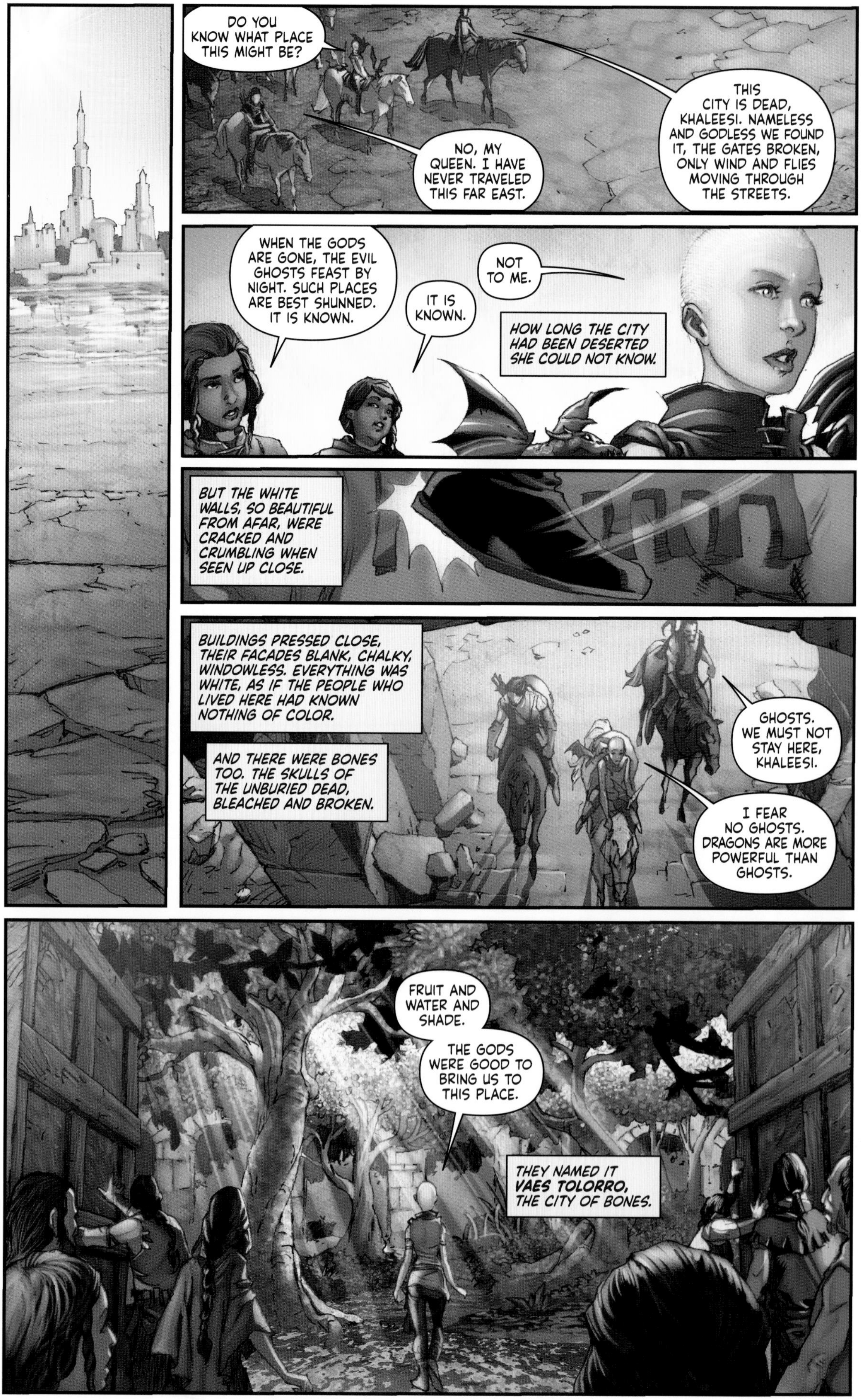

DO YOU KNOW WHAT PLACE THIS MIGHT BE?
NO, MY QUEEN. I HAVE NEVER TRAVELED THIS FAR EAST.
THIS CITY IS DEAD, KHALEESI. NAMELESS AND GODLESS WE FOUND IT, THE GATES BROKEN, ONLY WIND AND FLIES MOVING THROUGH THE STREETS.
WHEN THE GODS ARE GONE, THE EVIL GHOSTS FEAST BY NIGHT. SUCH PLACES ARE BEST SHUNNED. IT IS KNOWN.
IT IS KNOWN.
NOT TO ME.
HOW LONG THE CITY HAD BEEN DESERTED SHE COULD NOT KNOW.
BUT THE WHITE WALLS, SO BEAUTIFUL FROM AFAR, WERE CRACKED AND CRUMBLING WHEN SEEN UP CLOSE.
BUILDINGS PRESSED CLOSE, THEIR FACADES BLANK, CHALKY, WINDOWLESS. EVERYTHING WAS WHITE, AS IF THE PEOPLE WHO LIVED HERE HAD KNOWN NOTHING OF COLOR.
AND THERE WERE BONES TOO. THE SKULLS OF THE UNBURIED DEAD, BLEACHED AND BROKEN.
GHOSTS. WE MUST NOT STAY HERE, KHALEESI.
I FEAR NO GHOSTS. DRAGONS ARE MORE POWERFUL THAN GHOSTS.
FRUIT AND WATER AND SHADE.
THE GODS WERE GOOD TO BRING US TO THIS PLACE.
THEY NAMED IT **VAES TOLORRO,** THE CITY OF BONES.

KHALEESI... SIR JORAH WOULD SEE YOU.

SEND HIM IN, IRRI.

DANY HAD NAMED SER JORAH MORMONT THE FIRST OF HER QUEENSGUARD.

I'VE BROUGHT YOU A PEACH.

WE SHOULD REST HERE UNTIL WE ARE STRONGER. THE RED LANDS ARE NOT KIND TO THE WEAK.

IRRI AND JHIQUI SAY THERE ARE GHOSTS HERE.

THERE ARE GHOSTS EVERYWHERE. WE CARRY THEM WITH US WHEREVER WE GO.

TELL ME THE NAME OF YOUR GHOST, JORAH. YOU KNOW ALL OF MINE.

HER NAME WAS LYNESSE.

YOUR WIFE?

MY SECOND WIFE.

"MY HOME...YOU MUST UNDERSTAND THAT TO UNDERSTAND THE REST. BEAR ISLAND IS BEAUTIFUL, BUT REMOTE.

"THE ISLAND LIES FAR TO THE NORTH, AND OUR WINTERS ARE MORE TERRIBLE THAN YOU CAN IMAGINE, KHALEESI.

"I MARRIED YOUNG, TO A BRIDE OF MY FATHER'S CHOOSING. TEN YEARS WE WERE WED, AND I SUPPOSE I CAME TO LOVE HER AFTER A FASHION.

"THREE TIMES SHE MISCARRIED WHILE TRYING TO GIVE ME AN HEIR. THE LAST TIME SHE NEVER RECOVERED. SHE DIED NOT LONG AFTER.

"I FIGHT AS WELL AS ANY MAN, KHALEESI, BUT I HAVE NEVER BEEN A TOURNEY KNIGHT. YET WITH LYNESSE'S FAVOR KNOTTED ROUND MY ARM, I WAS A DIFFERENT MAN.

"I WON JOUST AFTER JOUST. I UNHORSED THEM ALL—EVEN SER BOROS BLOUNT OF THE KINGSGUARD.

"KING ROBERT GAVE ME THE CHAMPION'S LAUREL. I CROWNED LYNESSE QUEEN OF LOVE AND BEAUTY, AND THAT VERY NIGHT WENT TO HER FATHER AND ASKED FOR HER HAND.

"MY HOME WAS A GREAT DISAPPOINTMENT TO LYNESSE. IT WAS TOO COLD, TOO DAMP, TOO FAR AWAY, MY CASTLE NO MORE THAN A WOODEN LONGHALL.

"WE HAD NO MASQUES, NO BALLS OR FAIRS. SEASONS MIGHT PASS WITHOUT A SINGER EVER COMING, AND MY COOK KNEW LITTLE BEYOND HIS ROASTS AND STEWS.

"I LIVED FOR HER SMILES, SO WHATEVER SHE WANTED I FOUND FOR HER, BUT IT WAS NEVER ENOUGH. BEAR ISLAND IS RICH IN BEARS AND TREES BUT POOR IN AUGHT ELSE. I BORROWED HEAVILY FROM THE MONEYLENDERS.

"IT WAS AS A TOURNEY CHAMPION THAT I HAD WON HER HAND AND HEART, SO I ENTERED OTHER TOURNEYS FOR HER SAKE, BUT THE MAGIC WAS GONE.

"BY THEN MY FATHER HAD TAKEN THE BLACK, SO I WAS LORD OF BEAR ISLAND. I HAD NO LACK OF MARRIAGE OFFERS, BUT THEN LORD BALON GREYJOY ROSE IN REBELLION AGAINST THE USURPER, AND NED STARK CALLED HIS BANNERS TO HELP HIS FRIEND ROBERT.

"THE FINAL BATTLE WAS ON PYKE. WHEN ROBERT'S STONETHROWERS OPENED A BREACH IN KING BALON'S WALL, A PRIEST FROM MYR WAS THE FIRST MAN THROUGH, BUT I WAS NOT FAR BEHIND. FOR THAT I WON MY KNIGHTHOOD.

"TO CELEBRATE HIS VICTORY, ROBERT ORDAINED THAT A TOURNEY SHOULD BE HELD OUTSIDE LANNISPORT.

"IT WAS THERE I SAW LYNESSE, A MAID HALF MY AGE...

"BY RIGHTS I SHOULD HAVE GOTTEN A CONTEMPTUOUS REFUSAL, BUT LORD LEYTON ACCEPTED MY OFFER.

"WE WERE MARRIED THERE IN LANNISPORT, AND FOR A FORTNIGHT I WAS THE HAPPIEST MAN IN THE WIDE WORLD.

"FOR A FORTNIGHT WAS HOW LONG IT TOOK US TO SAIL FROM LANNISPORT BACK TO BEAR ISLAND.

"I NEVER DISTINGUISHED MYSELF AGAIN, AND EACH DEFEAT MEANT THE LOSS OF ANOTHER CHARGER AND ANOTHER SUIT OF JOUSTING ARMOR, WHICH MUST NEEDS BE RANSOMED OR REPLACED. THE COST COULD NOT BE BORNE.

"THE REST...I DID THINGS IT SHAMES ME TO SPEAK OF. FOR GOLD. SO LYNESSE MIGHT KEEP HER JEWELS, HER HARPER, AND HER COOK.

"IN THE END IT COST ME ALL. WHEN I HEARD THAT EDDARD STARK WAS COMING TO BEAR ISLAND, I WAS SO LOST TO HONOR THAT RATHER THAN STAY AND FACE HIS JUDGMENT, I TOOK HER WITH ME INTO EXILE.

"NOTHING MATTERED BUT OUR LOVE, I TOLD MYSELF. WE FLED TO LYS."

DID SHE DIE THERE?

ONLY TO ME.

IN HALF A YEAR MY REMAINING GOLD WAS GONE, AND I WAS OBLIGED TO TAKE SERVICE AS A SELLSWORD. WHILE I WAS FIGHTING BRAAVOSI ON THE RHOYNE, LYNESSE MOVED INTO THE MANSE OF A MERCHANT PRINCE NAMED TREGAR ORMOLLEN.

THEY SAY SHE IS HIS CHIEF CONCUBINE NOW, AND EVEN HIS WIFE GOES IN FEAR OF HER.

DO YOU HATE HER?

ALMOST AS MUCH AS I LOVE HER.

PRAY EXCUSE ME, MY QUEEN. I FIND I AM VERY TIRED.

JORAH...

WHAT DID SHE LOOK LIKE, YOUR LADY LYNESSE?

WHY, SHE LOOKED A BIT LIKE YOU, DAENERYS.

SLEEP WELL, MY QUEEN.

IT EXPLAINED MUCH THAT SHE HAD NOT TRULY UNDERSTOOD.

HE LOVES ME AS HE LOVED HER—NOT AS A KNIGHT LOVES HIS QUEEN, BUT AS A MAN LOVES A WOMAN.

SHE TRIED TO IMAGINE HERSELF IN SER JORAH'S ARMS, BUT IT WAS NO GOOD. WHEN SHE CLOSED HER EYES, HIS FACE KEPT CHANGING INTO DROGO'S.

HE CAN NEVER HAVE ME, BUT ONE DAY I CAN GIVE HIM BACK HIS HOME AND HONOR.

THAT MUCH I CAN DO FOR HIM.

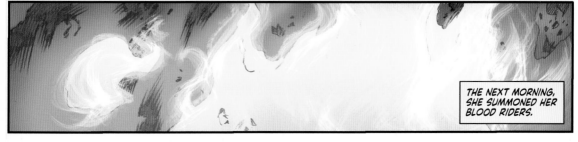

THE NEXT MORNING, SHE SUMMONED HER BLOOD RIDERS.

"BLOOD OF MY BLOOD," SHE TOLD THEM, "I HAVE NEED OF YOU. EACH OF YOU IS TO CHOOSE THREE HORSES, THE HARDIEST AND HEALTHIEST THAT REMAIN TO US.

"AGGO SHALL STRIKE SOUTHWEST, RAKHARO DUE SOUTH. JHOGO, YOU ARE TO FOLLOW **SHIERAK QIYA** ON SOUTHEAST.

"FIND OUT HOW FAR THIS WASTE EXTENDS BEFORE US, AND WHAT LIES ON THE OTHER SIDE."

AND SO THEY WENT, THE BELLS IN THEIR HAIR RINGING SOFTLY.

RAKHARO WAS THE FIRST TO RETURN.

DUE SOUTH THE RED WASTE STRETCHED ON AND ON, HE REPORTED, UNTIL IT ENDED ON A BLEAK SHORE BESIDE THE POISON WATER.

KHALEESI!

AGGO WAS BACK NEXT.

THE SOUTHWEST WAS BARREN AND BURNT, HE SWORE. HE HAD FOUND THE RUINS OF TWO MORE CITIES, SMALLER THAN VAES TOLORRO BUT OTHERWISE THE SAME.

JHOGO WAS GONE SO LONG THAT DANY FEARED HIM LOST, BUT FINALLY WHEN THEY HAD ALL BUT CEASED TO LOOK FOR HIM, HE CAME RIDING UP FROM THE SOUTHEAST.

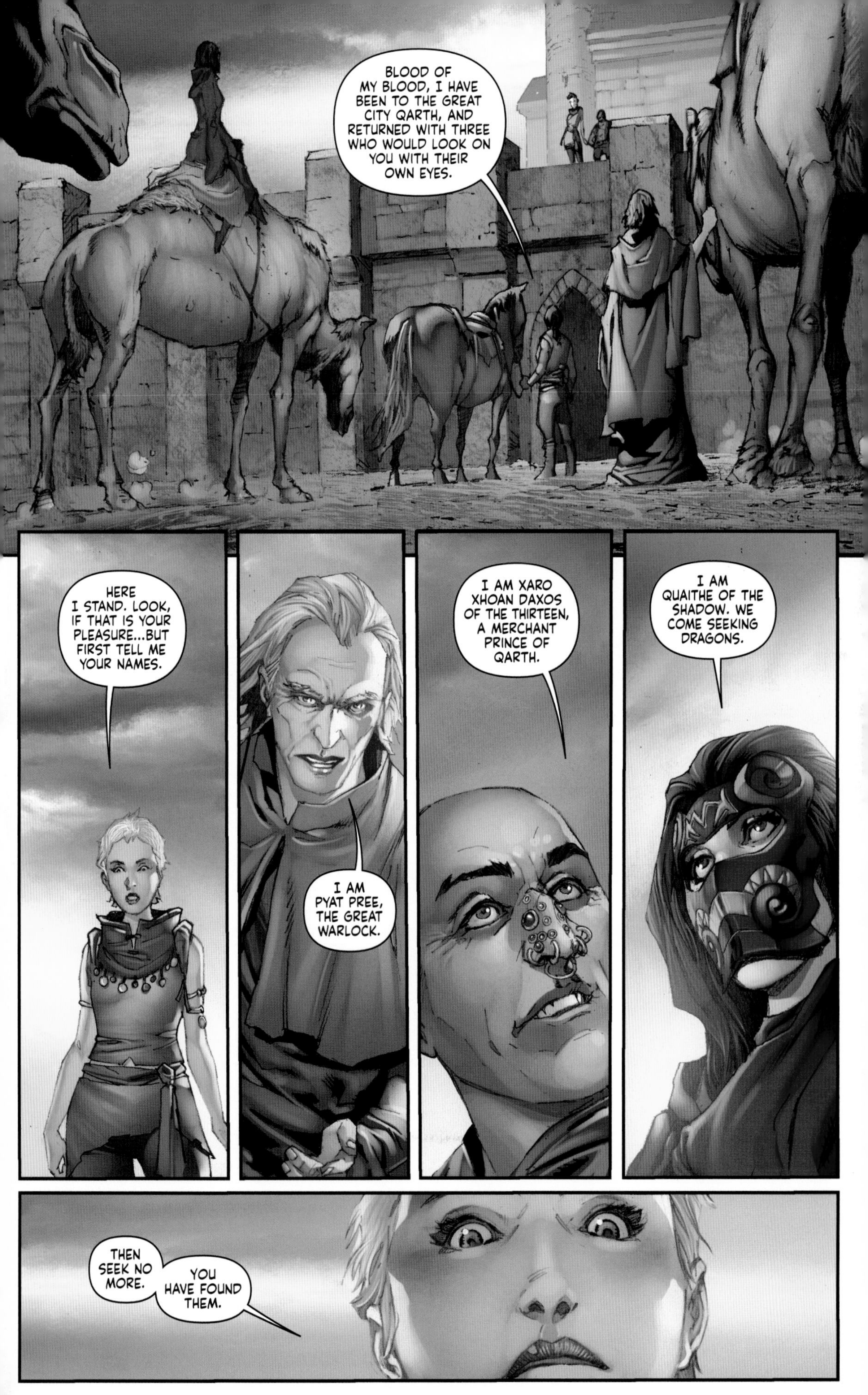
BLOOD OF MY BLOOD, I HAVE BEEN TO THE GREAT CITY QARTH, AND RETURNED WITH THREE WHO WOULD LOOK ON YOU WITH THEIR OWN EYES.
HERE I STAND. LOOK, IF THAT IS YOUR PLEASURE...BUT FIRST TELL ME YOUR NAMES.
I AM PYAT PREE, THE GREAT WARLOCK.
I AM XARO XHOAN DAXOS OF THE THIRTEEN, A MERCHANT PRINCE OF QARTH.
I AM QUAITHE OF THE SHADOW. WE COME SEEKING DRAGONS.
THEN SEEK NO MORE.
YOU HAVE FOUND THEM.

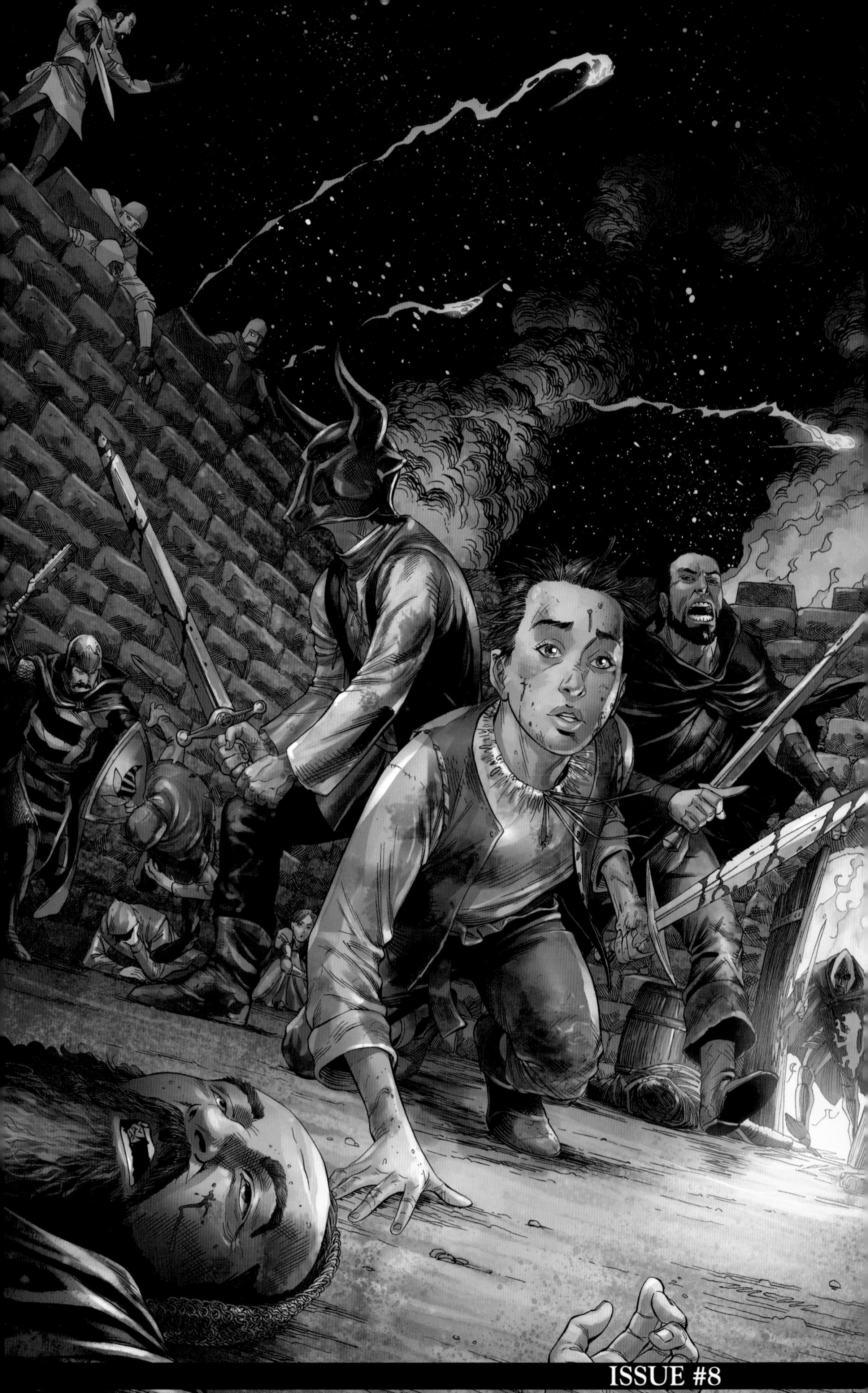

ISSUE #8

TREASON IS VILE ENOUGH, BUT THIS IS BAREFACED NAKED VILLAINY!

MAESTER FRENKEN RECEIVED THE FIRST MISSIVE AT CASTLE STOKEWORTH, YOUR GRACE. THE SECOND COPY CAME THROUGH LORD GYLES...

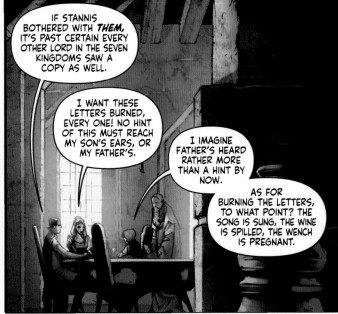

IF STANNIS BOTHERED WITH *THEM*, IT'S PAST CERTAIN EVERY OTHER LORD IN THE SEVEN KINGDOMS SAW A COPY AS WELL.

I WANT THESE LETTERS BURNED, EVERY ONE! NO HINT OF THIS MUST REACH MY SON'S EARS, OR MY FATHER'S.

I IMAGINE FATHER'S HEARD RATHER MORE THAN A HINT BY NOW.

AS FOR BURNING THE LETTERS, TO WHAT POINT? THE SONG IS SUNG, THE WINE IS SPILLED, THE WENCH IS PREGNANT.

I WILL NOT SUFFER TO BE CALLED A WHORE!

IT WAS ASTONISHING TO SEE HOW ANGRY CERSEI COULD WAX OVER ACCUSATIONS SHE KNEW PERFECTLY WELL TO BE TRUE. SHE OUGHT TO TAKE UP MUMMERY; SHE HAD A GIFT FOR IT.

THE COUNCIL MUST ISSUE AN EDICT. ANY MAN HEARD SPEAKING OF INCEST OR CALLING JOFF A BASTARD SHOULD LOSE HIS TONGUE!

A PRUDENT MEASURE.

A FOLLY. WHEN YOU TEAR OUT A MAN'S TONGUE, YOU ARE ONLY TELLING THE WORLD THAT YOU FEAR WHAT HE MIGHT SAY.

YOUR GRACE, YOUR BROTHER HAS THE RIGHT OF THIS. IF WE ATTEMPT TO SILENCE THIS TALK, WE ONLY LEND IT CREDENCE. BETTER TO TREAT IT WITH CONTEMPT, LIKE THE PATHETIC LIE IT IS.

AND MEANTIME, FIGHT FIRE WITH FIRE.

WHAT SORT OF FIRE?

A TALE OF SOMEWHAT THE SAME NATURE, PERHAPS. BUT MORE EASILY BELIEVED. LORD STANNIS HAS SPENT MOST OF HIS MARRIAGE APART FROM HIS WIFE. NOT THAT I FAULT HIM, I'D DO THE SAME WERE I MARRIED TO LADY SELYSE.

NONETHELESS, IF WE PUT IT ABOUT THAT HER DAUGHTER IS BASEBORN AND STANNIS A CUCKOLD, WELL...THE SMALLFOLK ARE ALWAYS EAGER TO BELIEVE THE WORST OF THEIR LORDS, PARTICULARLY THOSE AS STERN, SOUR, AND PRICKLY PROUD AS STANNIS BARATHEON.

HE HAS NEVER BEEN MUCH LOVED, THAT'S TRUE. SO WE PAY HIM BACK IN HIS OWN COIN. YES, I LIKE THIS.

BUT WHO CAN WE NAME AS LADY SELYSE'S LOVER? ONE OF HER UNCLES HAS BEEN WITH HER ON DRAGONSTONE ALL THIS TIME...

SER AXELL MIGHT SERVE FOR SHIREEN'S FATHER, BUT IN MY EXPERIENCE, THE MORE BIZARRE AND SHOCKING A TALE THE MORE APT IT IS TO BE REPEATED.

STANNIS KEEPS AN ESPECIALLY GROTESQUE FOOL, A LACKWIT WITH A TATTOOED FACE...ONE WHO IS UTTERLY DEVOTED TO THE GIRL AND FOLLOWS HER EVERYWHERE.

LORD PETYR, YOU ARE A WICKED CREATURE.

THANK YOU, YOUR GRACE.

AND A MOST ACCOMPLISHED LIAR.

WE ALL HAVE OUR GIFTS, MY LORD.

CUCKOLDED BY A HALFWIT FOOL! STANNIS WILL BE LAUGHED AT IN EVERY WINESINK THIS SIDE OF THE NARROW SEA.

WHORES LOVE TO GOSSIP, AND AS IT HAPPENS I OWN A BROTHEL OR THREE. AND NO DOUBT VARYS CAN PLANT SEEDS IN THE ALEHOUSES AND POT-SHOPS.

VARYS... WHERE *IS* VARYS?

I HAVE BEEN WONDERING THAT MYSELF, YOUR GRACE.

THE SPIDER SPINS HIS SECRET WEBS DAY AND NIGHT. I MISTRUST THAT ONE, MY LORDS.

AND HE SPEAKS SO KINDLY OF YOU.

AS IT HAPPENED, HE KNEW WHAT THE EUNUCH WAS ABOUT, BUT IT WAS NOTHING THE OTHER COUNCILLORS NEEDED TO HEAR.

PRAY EXCUSE ME, MY LORDS. OTHER BUSINESS CALLS.

KING'S BUSINESS?

WOULD YOU SPOIL MY SURPRISE? I'M HAVING A GIFT MADE FOR JOFFREY. A LITTLE CHAIN.

WHAT DOES HE NEED WITH ANOTHER CHAIN? HE HAS GOLD CHAINS AND SILVER, MORE THAN HE CAN WEAR. IF YOU THINK FOR A MOMENT YOU CAN BUY JOFF'S LOVE WITH GIFTS--

WHY, SURELY I *HAVE* THE KING'S LOVE, AS HE HAS MINE. AND *THIS* CHAIN I BELIEVE HE MAY ONE DAY TREASURE ABOVE ALL OTHERS.

IN HIS BEDCHAMBER, HE FOUND HIS SQUIRE LAYING OUT CLOTHING ON THE BED. PODRICK PAYNE WAS SO SHY HE WAS FURTIVE.

TYRION HAD NEVER QUITE GOTTEN OVER THE SUSPICION THAT HIS FATHER HAD INFLICTED THE BOY ON HIM AS A JOKE.

TYRION LANNISTER, HAND OF THE KING.

GOODMEN, I KNOW YOU ARE ALL BUSY, SO I WILL BE SUCCINCT. POD, IF YOU PLEASE.

I HAD THESE MADE AT THE CASTLE FORGE. I WANT A THOUSAND MORE JUST LIKE THEM.

THUNK

A MIGHTY CHAIN.

MIGHTY, BUT SHORT. SOMEWHAT LIKE ME. I FANCY ONE A GOOD DEAL LONGER. DO YOU HAVE A NAME?

THEY CALL ME IRONBELLY, M'LORD.

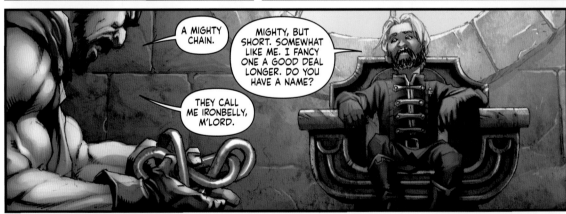

I WANT EVERY FORGE IN KING'S LANDING TURNED TO MAKING THESE LINKS AND JOINING THEM. ALL OTHER WORK IS TO BE PUT ASIDE.

WHEN I RIDE UP THE STREET OF STEEL, I WANT TO HEAR HAMMERS RINGING, NIGHT OR DAY. AND I WANT A MAN, A STRONG MAN, TO SEE THAT ALL THIS IS DONE. ARE YOU THAT MAN, GOODMAN IRONBELLY?

MIGHT BE I AM, M'LORD. BUT WHAT OF THE MAIL AND SWORDS THE QUEEN WAS WANTING?

THAT WORK CAN WAIT. THE CHAIN FIRST.

M'LORD, BEGGING YOUR PARDON, HER GRACE SAID THOSE AS DIDN'T MEET THEIR NUMBERS WOULD HAVE THEIR HANDS CRUSHED. SMASHED ON THEIR OWN ANVILS, SHE SAID.

NO ONE WILL HAVE THEIR HANDS SMASHED. YOU HAVE MY WORD ON IT.

MY LORD, THIS IS CRUDE WORK AT BEST. THERE IS NO ART TO IT.

I AM A MASTER ARMORER, AS IT PLEASE MY LORD. THIS IS NO WORK FOR ME, NOR MY FELLOW MASTERS. WE MAKE SWORDS AS SHARP AS SONG, ARMOR SUCH AS A GOD MIGHT WEAR.

NOT *THIS.*

WHAT IS YOUR NAME, MASTER ARMORER?

SALLOREON. AND IF THE KING'S HAND WILL PERMIT, I SHOULD BE *MOST* HONORED TO FORGE HIM A SUIT OF ARMOR SUITABLE TO HIS HOUSE AND HIGH OFFICE.

MASTER SALLOREON, I PLAN TO FIGHT THE REST OF MY BATTLES FROM THIS CHAIR. IT'S LINKS I NEED, NOT ARMOR.

SO LET ME PUT IT TO YOU THIS WAY. YOU WILL MAKE CHAINS, OR YOU WILL WEAR THEM.

THE CHOICE IS YOURS.

YOU KNOW WHERE WE'RE BOUND.

HE HAD DONE ALL HE COULD TO FEED THE HUNGRY CITY.

HE'D SET SEVERAL HUNDRED CARPENTERS TO BUILDING FISHING BOATS IN PLACE OF CATAPULTS, OPENED THE KINGSWOOD TO ANY HUNTER WHO DARED TO CROSS THE RIVER.

HE HAD EVEN SENT GOLD CLOAKS FORAGING TO THE WEST AND SOUTH...

...YET HE STILL SAW ACCUSING EYES EVERYWHERE HE RODE.

LEAVE ONE MAN HERE WHO'LL KNOW WHERE TO FIND THE OTHERS WHEN I WISH TO RETURN.

AS YOU SAY.

I AM CHATAYA. AND THIS IS MY DAUGHTER, ALAYAYA.

COME, MY LORD.

YOU ARE VERY BEAUTIFUL, ALAYAYA. FROM HEAD TO HEELS, EVERY PART OF YOU IS LOVELY.

YET JUST NOW THE PART THAT INTERESTS ME MOST IS YOUR TONGUE.

MY LORD WILL FIND MY TONGUE WELL SCHOOLED. WHEN I WAS A GIRL I LEARNED WHEN TO USE IT, AND WHEN NOT.

THAT PLEASES ME. SO WHAT SHALL WE DO NOW? PERCHANCE YOU HAVE SOME SUGGESTION?

YES. IF MY LORD WILL OPEN THE WARDROBE, HE WILL FIND WHAT HE SEEKS.

VARYS.

WAS CHATAYA'S TO YOUR SATISFACTION, MY LORD?

ALMOST TOO MUCH SO. YOU'RE CERTAIN THIS WOMAN CAN BE RELIED ON?

I AM CERTAIN OF NOTHING IN THIS FICKLE AND TREACHEROUS WORLD, MY LORD.

EVEN VARYS'S WALK WAS DIFFERENT. THE SCENT OF SOUR WINE AND GARLIC CLUNG TO HIM INSTEAD OF LAVENDER.

I LIKE THIS NEW GARB OF YOURS.

THE WORK I DO DOES NOT PERMIT ME TO TRAVEL THE STREETS AMID A COLUMN OF KNIGHTS. SO WHEN I LEAVE THE CASTLE, I ADOPT MORE SUITABLE GUISES, AND THUS LIVE TO SERVE YOU LONGER.

LEATHER BECOMES YOU. YOU OUGHT TO COME LIKE THIS TO OUR NEXT COUNCIL SESSION.

YOUR SISTER WOULD NOT APPROVE, MY LORD.

MY SISTER WOULD SOIL HER SMALLCLOTHES. I SAW NO SIGNS OF ANY OF HER SPIES SKULKING AFTER ME.

MEN SEE WHAT THEY EXPECT TO SEE.

DWARFS ARE NOT SO COMMON A SIGHT AS CHILDREN, SO A CHILD IS WHAT THEY WILL SEE. A BOY IN AN OLD CLOAK ON HIS FATHER'S HORSE, GOING ABOUT HIS FATHER'S BUSINESS. THOUGH IT WOULD BE BEST IF YOU CAME MOST OFTEN BY NIGHT.

I AM PLEASED TO HEAR IT, MY LORD. SOME OF YOUR SISTER'S HIRELINGS ARE MINE AS WELL, UNBEKNOWNST TO HER. I SHOULD HATE TO THINK THEY HAD GROWN SO SLOPPY AS TO BE SEEN.

IF YOU WILL PERMIT ME?

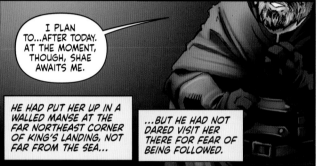

I PLAN TO...AFTER TODAY. AT THE MOMENT, THOUGH, SHAE AWAITS ME.

HE HAD PUT HER UP IN A WALLED MANSE AT THE FAR NORTHEAST CORNER OF KING'S LANDING, NOT FAR FROM THE SEA...

...BUT HE HAD NOT DARED VISIT HER THERE FOR FEAR OF BEING FOLLOWED.

YOU MISSED A LIVELY COUNCIL. STANNIS HAS CROWNED HIMSELF, IT SEEMS.

I KNOW.

HE ACCUSES MY BROTHER AND SISTER OF INCEST. I WONDER HOW HE CAME BY THAT SUSPICION.

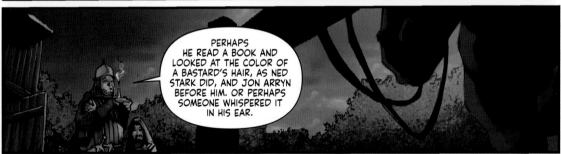

PERHAPS HE READ A BOOK AND LOOKED AT THE COLOR OF A BASTARD'S HAIR, AS NED STARK DID, AND JON ARRYN BEFORE HIM. OR PERHAPS SOMEONE WHISPERED IT IN HIS EAR.

SOMEONE LIKE YOU, PERCHANCE?

AM I SUSPECTED? IT WAS NOT ME. BESIDES, THE BASTARDS WERE THERE FOR ALL TO SEE.

ROBERT'S BASTARDS? WHAT OF THEM?

HE FATHERED EIGHT, TO THE BEST OF MY KNOWING.

THEIR MOTHERS WERE COPPER AND HONEY, CHESTNUT AND BUTTER, YET THE BABES WERE ALL BLACK AS RAVENS...AND AS ILL-OMENED, IT WOULD SEEM.

SO WHEN JOFFREY, MYRCELLA, AND TOMMEN SLID OUT BETWEEN YOUR SISTER'S THIGHS, EACH AS GOLDEN AS THE SUN, THE TRUTH WAS NOT HARD TO GLIMPSE.

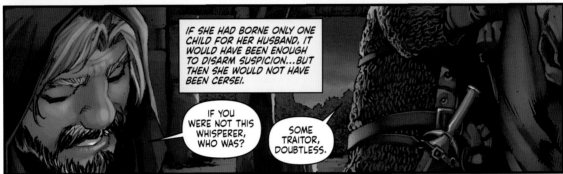

IF SHE HAD BORNE ONLY ONE CHILD FOR HER HUSBAND, IT WOULD HAVE BEEN ENOUGH TO DISARM SUSPICION...BUT THEN SHE WOULD NOT HAVE BEEN CERSEI.

IF YOU WERE NOT THIS WHISPERER, WHO WAS?

SOME TRAITOR, DOUBTLESS.

LITTLEFINGER?

I NAMED NO NAME.

LORD VARYS...SOMETIMES I FEEL AS THOUGH YOU ARE THE BEST FRIEND I HAVE IN KING'S LANDING, AND SOMETIMES I FEEL YOU ARE MY WORST ENEMY.

HOW ODD. I THINK QUITE THE SAME OF YOU.

ARYA

BECAUSE OF THE RIVER, THEY COULDN'T GO AROUND WEST OF THE LAKE, LIKE YOREN HAD THOUGHT. AND EAST WOULD TAKE THEM BACK TO THE KINGSROAD.

YOREN REMEMBERED A TOWN. A HOLDFAST WITH A TOWER.

BUT THE TOWN WAS ABANDONED, AND THE TOWER WAS EMPTY.

ARRY'S SCARED!

I'M NOT, BUT *THEY* WERE.

HUU... WHUUUHU...

SMART BOY. THING IS, THE FOLKS WHO LIVED HERE WERE AT WAR, LIKE IT OR NO. WE'RE NOT. NIGHT'S WATCH TAKES NO PART, SO NO MAN'S OUR ENEMY.

GODS BE GOOD, THERE'S STILL A BOAT HERE. WE'LL FIND A WIND AND SAIL ACROSS THE GODS EYE TO HARRENTOWN.

WE CAN BUY NEW MOUNTS THERE, OR ELSE TAKE SHELTER AT HARRENHAL. THAT'S LADY WHENT'S SEAT, AND SHE'S ALWAYS BEEN A FRIEND O' THE WATCH.

WE SHOULDN'T STAY HERE. THE PEOPLE DIDN'T. THEY ALL RAN OFF, EVEN THEIR LORD.

THERE'S GHOSTS IN HARRENHAL!

ARYA REMEMBERED THE STORIES OLD NAN USED TO TELL OF HARRENHAL.

NAN SAID THAT FIERY SPIRITS STILL HAUNTED THE BLACKENED TOWERS. SOMETIMES MEN WENT TO SLEEP IN THEIR BEDS AND WERE FOUND DEAD IN THE MORNING, ALL BURNT UP.

THERE'S FOR YOUR GHOSTS.

BUT ARYA DIDN'T REALLY BELIEVE THAT, AND HOT PIE WAS BEING SILLY. IT WOULDN'T BE GHOSTS AT HARRENHAL...

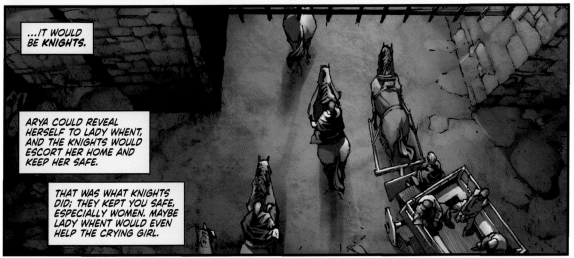

...IT WOULD BE *KNIGHTS*.

ARYA COULD REVEAL HERSELF TO LADY WHENT, AND THE KNIGHTS WOULD ESCORT HER HOME AND KEEP HER SAFE.

THAT WAS WHAT KNIGHTS DID; THEY KEPT YOU SAFE, ESPECIALLY WOMEN. MAYBE LADY WHENT WOULD EVEN HELP THE CRYING GIRL.

THEY EXPLORED THE HOLDFAST FROM TOP TO BOTTOM.

THEY SECURED THE GATE, AND BLOCKED THE TRAP THEY FOUND UNDER THE STRAW OF AN OLD BARN.

GERREN FOLLOWED IT A LONG WAY UNDER THE EARTH AND CAME OUT BY THE LAKE.

YOREN HAD THEM ROLL A WAGON ON TOP OF THE TRAP, TO MAKE CERTAIN NO ONE CAME IN THAT WAY.

BUT THERE WERE NO BOATS.

AS SHE CURLED UP ON HER PALLET FOR THE NIGHT, ARYA COULD HEAR THE CRYING GIRL FROM THE FAR SIDE OF THE HOLDFAST.

SHE WISHED THE GIRL WOULD JUST BE QUIET. WHY DID SHE HAVE TO CRY ALL THE TIME?

AAAH!

WOTH, GENDRY, DIDN'T YOU HEAR?

HOT PIE, WAKE UP!

...HH?

WHAT'S WRONG?

HEAR WHAT?

ARRY HAD A BAD DREAM.

NO, I HEARD IT. A WOLF.

LET THEM HOWL. THEY'RE OUT THERE, WE'RE IN HERE.

NEVER SAW NO WOLF COULD STORM A HOLDFAST.

I NEVER HEARD NOTHING.

IT WAS A *WOLF!* SOMETHING'S WRONG!

BEEEEEEHHWWWRRRRR

THE HORN...

SOMEONE'S COMING! GET UP!

SHE SCRAMBLED UP
ONTO THE CATWALK.

THE PARAPETS WERE A
BIT TOO HIGH AND ARYA A
BIT TOO SHORT; SHE HAD
TO WEDGE HER TOES INTO
THE HOLES BETWEEN THE
STONES TO SEE OVER.

FOR A MOMENT SHE THOUGHT
THE TOWN WAS FULL OF LANTERN
BUGS. THEN SHE REALIZED THEY
WERE MEN WITH TORCHES,
GALLOPING BETWEEN THE HOUSES.

SHE SAW A ROOF GO UP, FLAMES
LICKING AT THE BELLY OF THE NIGHT
WITH HOT ORANGE TONGUES AS THE
THATCH CAUGHT. ANOTHER FOLLOWED,
AND THEN ANOTHER, AND SOON THERE
WERE FIRES BLAZING EVERYWHERE.

A COLUMN OF RIDERS MOVED BETWEEN
THE BURNING BUILDINGS TOWARD THE
HOLDFAST. FIRELIGHT GLITTERED OFF
METAL HELMS AND SPATTERED THEIR
MAIL AND PLATE WITH ORANGE AND
YELLOW HIGHLIGHTS.

ONE CARRIED A BANNER ON A TALL
LANCE. SHE THOUGHT IT WAS RED,
BUT IT WAS HARD TO TELL IN THE
NIGHT, WITH THE FIRES ROARING
ALL AROUND. EVERYTHING SEEMED
RED OR BLACK OR ORANGE.

THE FIRE LEAPT FROM ONE HOUSE
TO ANOTHER. ARYA SAW A TREE
CONSUMED, THE FLAMES CREEPING
ACROSS ITS BRANCHES UNTIL IT
STOOD AGAINST THE NIGHT IN
ROBES OF LIVING ORANGE.

EVERYONE WAS AWAKE NOW,
MANNING THE CATWALKS OR
STRUGGLING WITH THE
FRIGHTENED ANIMALS BELOW.

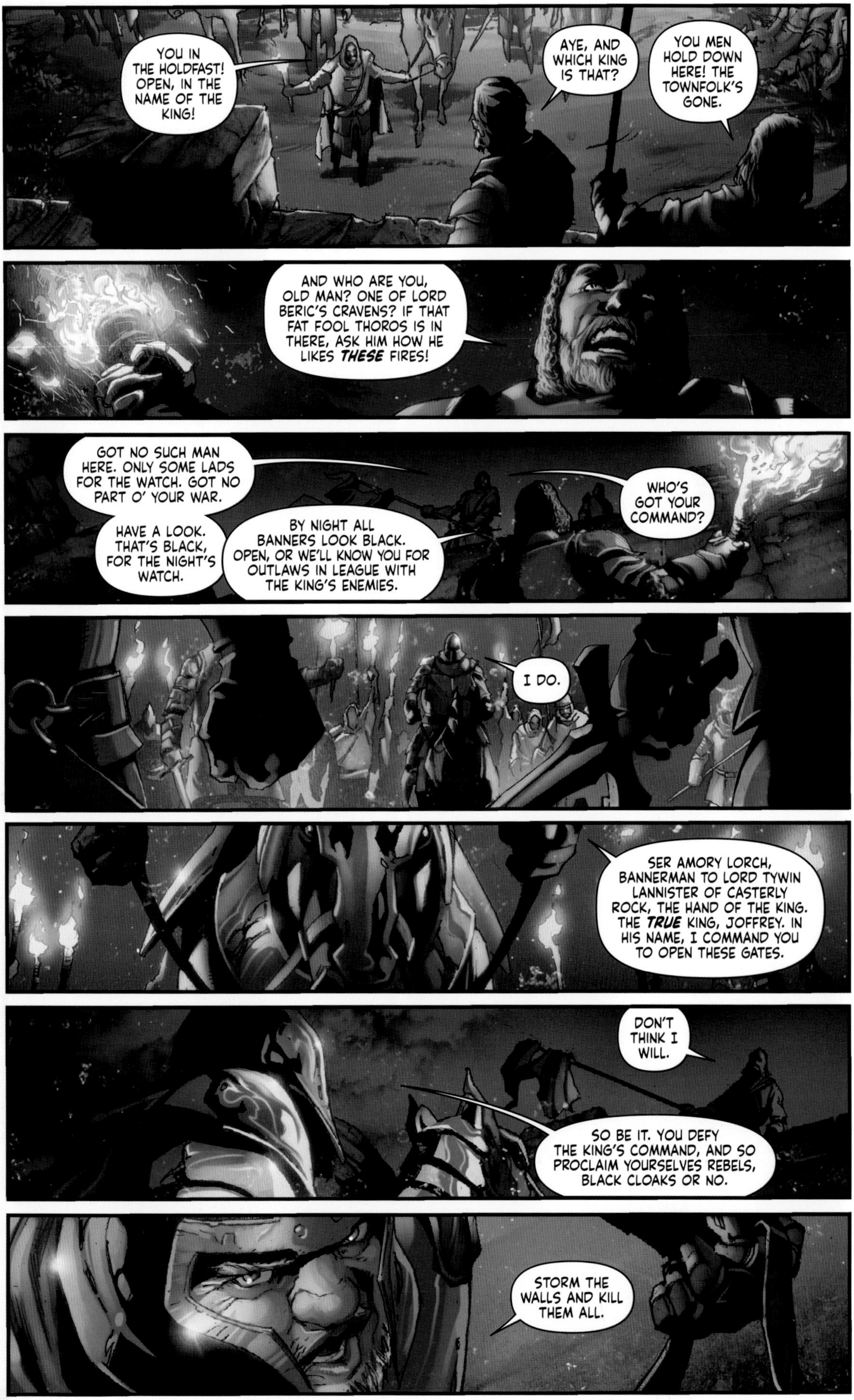
YOU IN THE HOLDFAST! OPEN, IN THE NAME OF THE KING!
AYE, AND WHICH KING IS THAT?
YOU MEN HOLD DOWN HERE! THE TOWNFOLK'S GONE.
AND WHO ARE YOU, OLD MAN? ONE OF LORD BERIC'S CRAVENS? IF THAT FAT FOOL THOROS IS IN THERE, ASK HIM HOW HE LIKES *THESE* FIRES!
GOT NO SUCH MAN HERE. ONLY SOME LADS FOR THE WATCH. GOT NO PART O' YOUR WAR.
HAVE A LOOK. THAT'S BLACK, FOR THE NIGHT'S WATCH.
BY NIGHT ALL BANNERS LOOK BLACK. OPEN, OR WE'LL KNOW YOU FOR OUTLAWS IN LEAGUE WITH THE KING'S ENEMIES.
WHO'S GOT YOUR COMMAND?
I DO.
SER AMORY LORCH, BANNERMAN TO LORD TYWIN LANNISTER OF CASTERLY ROCK, THE HAND OF THE KING. THE *TRUE* KING, JOFFREY. IN HIS NAME, I COMMAND YOU TO OPEN THESE GATES.
DON'T THINK I WILL.
SO BE IT. YOU DEFY THE KING'S COMMAND, AND SO PROCLAIM YOURSELVES REBELS, BLACK CLOAKS OR NO.
STORM THE WALLS AND KILL THEM ALL.

BLADES! SPREAD APART, DEFEND THE WALL WHEREVER THEY HIT!

WINTERFELL!

FOR EACH ONE ARYA CUT OR STABBED OR SHOVED BACK, ANOTHER WAS COMING OVER THE WALL.

AAAH!

RRHHH!

ARYA SAW A GOLD LION ON A RED BANNER AND THOUGHT OF JOFFREY, WISHING HE WAS HERE SO SHE COULD DRIVE NEEDLE THOUGH HIS SNEERY FACE.

EVERYTHING SMELLED OF BLOOD AND SMOKE AND IRON AND PISS...

HOT PIE!

...BUT AFTER A TIME IT SEEMED LIKE THAT WAS ONLY ONE SMELL.

SER AMORY HAD NO LADDERS, BUT THE HOLDFAST WALLS WERE ROUGH-CUT AND UNMORTARED, EASY TO CLIMB, AND THERE SEEMED TO BE NO END TO THE FOES.

GHHK!

EVERY TIME ARYA LOOKED UP, MORE TORCHES WERE FLYING, TRAILING LONG TONGUES OF FLAME THAT LINGERED BEHIND HER EYES.

THERE WERE STEEL SHADOWS RUNNING THROUGH THE HOLDFAST, FIRELIGHT SHINING ON MAIL AND BLADES.

THE NIGHT RANG TO THE CLASH OF STEEL AND THE CRIES OF THE WOUNDED AND DYING.

FOR A MOMENT ARYA STOOD UNCERTAIN, NOT KNOWING WHICH WAY TO GO.

DEATH WAS ALL AROUND HER.

BOY! GET **OUT**, IT'S DONE, WE'VE LOST. HERD UP ALL YOU CAN, THE BOYS, YOU GET THEM OUT. **NOW!**

HOW?

THAT TRAP! UNDER THE BARN!

HE SAID *GO!* THE BARN, THE WAY OUT!

COME ON...

THE FIRE WAS SPREADING FASTER THAN SHE WOULD HAVE BELIEVED. ARYA REMEMBERED THE HOUND'S HORRIBLE BURNED FACE.

HHHUUUWHHH...

ARRY, LEAVE HER IF SHE WON'T COME!

RUN!

HHHWWHUUHUHU...

GOOD BOYS, KIND BOYS!

GET THESE FUCKING CHAINS OFF!

THERE'S NO TIME.

YOU TAKE HER! YOU GET HER OUT! YOU DO IT!

THE FIRE BEAT AT HER BACK WITH HOT RED WINGS AS SHE FLED THE BURNING BARN.

IT FELT BLESSEDLY COOL OUTSIDE, BUT MEN WERE DYING ALL AROUND HER. SMOKE WAS EVERYWHERE.

GGH!

GOING BACK INTO THAT BARN WAS THE HARDEST THING SHE HAD EVER DONE. SMOKE WAS POURING OUT THE OPEN DOOR LIKE A WRITHING BLACK SNAKE.

SHE COULD HEAR THE SCREAMS OF THE POOR ANIMALS INSIDE, DONKEYS AND HORSES AND MEN.

THE WAGON JUMPED HALF A FOOT WHEN BITER THREW HIMSELF AGAINST HIS CHAINS AGAIN.

ARYA HEARD THE STEEL CRASH THROUGH THE OLD WOOD, AND AGAIN, AGAIN.

AN INSTANT LATER CAME A **CRACK** AS LOUD AS THUNDER, AND THE BOTTOM OF THE WAGON CAME RIPPING LOOSE IN AN EXPLOSION OF SPLINTERS.

AAH!

ARYA ROLLED HEADFIRST INTO THE TUNNEL AND DROPPED FIVE FEET. SHE GOT DIRT IN HER MOUTH BUT SHE DIDN'T CARE.

THE TASTE WAS FINE, THE TASTE WAS MUD AND WATER AND WORMS AND LIFE.

A DOZEN FEET DOWN THE TUNNEL SHE HEARD THE SOUND, LIKE THE ROAR OF SOME MONSTROUS BEAST, AND A CLOUD OF HOT SMOKE AND BLACK DUST CAME BILLOWING UP BEHIND HER, SMELLING OF HELL.

HFF!

UNDER THE EARTH THE AIR WAS COOL AND DARK. ABOVE WAS NOTHING BUT BLOOD AND ROARING RED AND CHOKING SMOKE AND THE SCREAMS OF DYING HORSES.

HH... HUHHHH...

HHUUUH... UUUHUHHUH...

ARYA HELD HER BREATH AND KISSED THE MUD ON THE FLOOR OF THE TUNNEL AND CRIED...

...BUT FOR WHOM, SHE COULD NOT SAY.

COVER GALLERY

ISSUE #1 COVER B
Art by Magali Villeneuve

ISSUE #1 COVER C
Art by Marc Simonetti

ISSUE #1   COVER D
DYNAMITE's subscription variant
Art by Mel Rubi   Colors by Omi Remalante, Jr.

ISSUE #2   COVER B
DYNAMITE's subscription variant
Art by Mel Rubi   Colors by Omi Remalante, Jr.

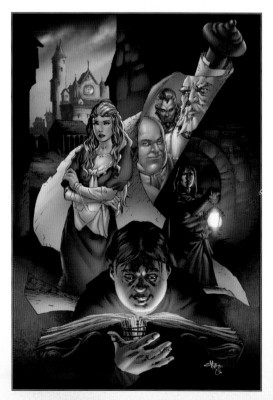

ISSUE #3   COVER B
DYNAMITE's subscription variant
Art by Mel Rubi   Colors by Omi Remalante, Jr.

ISSUE #4   COVER B
DYNAMITE's subscription variant
Art by Mel Rubi   Colors by Omi Remalante, Jr.

ISSUE #5　COVER B
DYNAMITE's subscription variant
Art by Mel Rubi　Colors by Omi Remalante, Jr.

ISSUE #6　COVER B
DYNAMITE's subscription variant
Art by Mel Rubi　Colors by Omi Remalante, Jr.

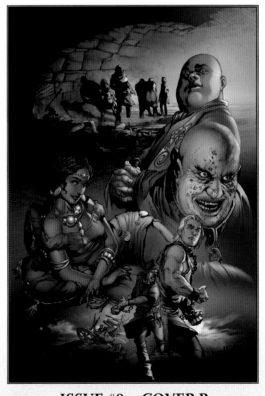

ISSUE #7　COVER B
DYNAMITE's subscription variant
Art by Mel Rubi　Colors by Omi Remalante, Jr.

ISSUE #8　COVER B
DYNAMITE's subscription variant
Art by Mel Rubi　Colors by Omi Remalante, Jr.

GEORGE R. R. MARTIN is the #1 *New York Times* bestselling author of many novels, including those of the acclaimed series A Song of Ice and Fire—*A Game of Thrones, A Clash of Kings, A Storm of Swords, A Feast for Crows*, and *A Dance with Dragons* as well as *Tuf Voyaging, Fevre Dream, The Armageddon Rag, Dying of the Light, Windhaven* (with Lisa Tuttle), and *Dreamsongs Volumes I* and *II*. He is also the creator of *The Lands of Ice and Fire,* a collection of maps from A Song of Ice and Fire featuring original artwork from illustrator and cartographer Jonathan Roberts as well as *The World of Ice & Fire* with Elio M. García, Jr., and Linda Antonsson. As a writer-producer, he has worked on *The Twilight Zone, Beauty and the Beast,* and various feature films and pilots that were never made. He lives with the lovely Parris in Santa Fe, New Mexico.

georgerrmartin.com
Facebook.com/GeorgeRRMartinofficial
Twitter: @GRRMspeaking

LANDRY Q. WALKER is a *New York Times* bestselling author of comics and books. He lives with his cats and his wife, and he spends his days pushing buttons randomly on a keyboard until stories somehow happen.

MEL RUBI has been a professional artist since 1993, and enjoys challenging himself on every difficult task he takes on. He loves playing chess and is a family man.
melrubi.com

IVAN NUNES has been a professional colorist since 2006, having made approximately 200 comic books, mostly by Dynamite, and more than 900 covers. He is currently working on *A Clash of Kings* for Dynamite and *Action Comics* for DC Comics.
Facebook.com/ivan.nunes.73

SIMON BOWLAND has been lettering comics since 2004, producing work for all of the mainstream publishers in both the UK and the United States. He lives in England alongside his partner, Pippa, and their cat, and dedicates his work on this book to the memory of his beloved mother, Annette.
Twitter: @SimonBowland